A minute after Cassie had finished applying a light coat of make-up her door buzzer echoed through the apartment.

Her heart stuttered, and her stomach clenched with nerves, but she went over to the intercom to let him in.

He knocked at the door barely a minute later and she looped her purse over her shoulder before walking over to open the door. "Good morning," she greeted him. "I'm ready."

His blue eyes swept over her, glinting with approval. "You look amazing, Cassandra," he murmured.

She licked her suddenly dry lips. "Thanks," she murmured. "So do you." Oh, boy, what was wrong with her? She was acting as if this was a *date*.

His gaze held hers for a long second, as if he were remembering their brief kiss. Or maybe that was just *her* memory working overtime. He stepped back, giving her room to leave her apartment. She released her pent-up breath and wondered if she was crazy to spend her day off with Ryan.

She liked him too much already. And she couldn't bear the ~~power to~~ hurt her.

No, sh~~~~ become emotion~~~~ called him T~~~~

Dear Reader,

As many of you know, I am a nurse by background and still work full-time at our local hospital.

Recently I was involved in a 'Safe Haven' baby situation. A young woman who gave birth at our hospital decided she couldn't be a good mother and wanted to give her baby up for adoption. So far the State of Wisconsin has had eighty-four Safe Haven babies since the law was passed in 1994.

The situation I was involved in was very different from the one I describe in this story, *Wanted: Parents for a Baby!*, but the idea of writing my own Medical Romance about a Safe Haven baby kept popping into my head, nagging at me, until I simply had to sit down and put my ideas on paper. In some ways I think this book wrote itself!

I hope you enjoy Ryan and Cassie's story as much as I do—and please drop by to visit my website at www.lauraiding.com if you have a moment. I always enjoy hearing from my readers.

Happy reading!

Laura Iding

WANTED: PARENTS FOR A BABY!

BY
LAURA IDING

MILLS & BOON

Published in Great Britain 2015
by Mills & Boon, an imprint of Harlequin (UK) Limited,
Eton House, 18-24 Paradise Road, Richmond, Surrey, TW9 1SR

© 2015 Laura Iding

ISBN: 978-0-263-24701-5

Harlequin (UK) Limited's policy is to use papers that are natural,
renewable and recyclable products and made from wood grown in
sustainable forests. The logging and manufacturing processes conform
to the legal environmental regulations of the country of origin.

Printed and bound in Spain
by CPI, Barcelona

Laura Iding loved reading as a child, and when she ran out of books she readily made up her own, completing a little detective mini-series when she was twelve. But when her parents insisted she get a 'real' career she turned to nursing—another truly rewarding job. After thirty years of experience in trauma/critical care, she's thrilled to combine her career and her hobby into one—writing Medical Romances™ for Mills & Boon®. Laura lives in the northern part of the United States with her husband of nearly thirty years, and spends her time reading, writing and biking.

Books by Laura Iding

NYC Angels: Unmasking Dr Serious
Her Little Spanish Secret
Dating Dr Delicious
A Knight for Nurse Hart
The Nurse's Brooding Boss
The Surgeon's New-Year Wedding Wish
Expecting a Christmas Miracle

**Visit the author profile page
at millsandboon.co.uk for more titles**

This book is dedicated to Michelle Lahey Reed, an amazing woman who opened her heart and her home to foster twin babies in need. You are truly an inspiration!

CHAPTER ONE

"Cassie?" Alice, the neonatal intensive care unit clerk, called across the unit. "The ER is asking you to come down with the emergency warmer."

"Really?" Neonatal nurse Cassandra Jordan glanced up from her computer in surprise. This was an interesting way to start her shift, and it was only Thursday. The unusual stuff mostly happened on the weekends. "Is there a pregnant woman waiting?"

"Not sure, but they asked you to hurry."

Cassie nodded and quickly abandoned her charting, heading over to where they kept the portable warmer stocked with emergency equipment. "What about a physician?" she asked as she wheeled the warmer toward the door.

"Already paged him. Dr. Ryan should be there soon."

Cassie's stomach clenched with a mixture of dread and anticipation even as she tipped her head to indicate she understood. After wheeling the infant warmer into the hallway, she pushed the button for the elevator, relieved when the doors immediately opened.

Dr. Ryan Murphy was one of the best neonatal intensivists she'd ever worked with. Unfortunately, he was far too tall, dark and handsome for her peace of mind.

Not to mention single. Widowed, to be exact. According to the gossip mill, he wasn't interested in dating, much to the dismay of the single nurses working throughout the hospital.

To be fair, she wasn't particularly interested in dating either—one deep betrayal and subsequent failed marriage had been enough to put her off men for a long time. But somehow in the six months that she'd been in Cedar Bluff, her body hadn't seemed to get the message. Every time Dr. Ryan's penetrating blue eyes met hers, her stomach did a series of backward flips and she blushed like a fool. She mentally cursed her fair skin for constantly betraying her.

The elevator doors dinged and opened on the ground level, so she wheeled the warmer out and quickly jogged down the hall to Cedar Bluff's ER. There was a crowd of people gathered around the triage desk and, of course, Dr. Ryan's dark head, clearly visible above the crowd, drew her gaze like a magnet. Even wearing blue scrubs and long white lab coat, he was distinctly noticeable.

He glanced over and caught sight of her, acknowledging her presence with a brief nod. He made a gesture with his hand. "Please, step back and make room for the equipment."

Like the parting of the Red Sea, the group of people split down the middle to give Cassie the access she needed. She focused on the infant car seat that was propped on the desktop and frowned as she registered the fact that the baby was letting out a terrible high-pitched cry. "What happened? Where's the mother?"

"She left," Dr. Ryan said shortly. "This little girl is only a day or two old and desperately needs medical care. We need to get her in the warmer so I can examine her."

"Her name is Emma," Gloria, the ER nurse at the triage desk, supplied helpfully. "The mother said she was unfit and asked me to take care of Emma."

Pretty name, Cassie thought as she quickly plugged in the warmer and turned on the heat lamps. She cracked open the oxygen tank and connected the tubing while Dr. Ryan lifted the tiny infant from the car seat. He set her gently in the center of the warmer, and the baby's arms and legs flailed about in protest.

Emma's high-pitched cry wasn't easy to ignore, but Cassie focused on setting up the open end of the oxygen tubing so it would gently stream past her tiny nose and mouth. Dr. Ryan undressed the baby, who was wearing clean yet well-worn clothing, his fingers looking ridiculously large in contrast to the tiny baby. Using his stethoscope, he listened to Emma's heart and lungs. Cassie placed small EKG patches on the baby's bare chest and their fingers brushed as they both worked over the small torso.

Cassie ignored the tingling sensation that rippled up her arms at his touch and peered at the cardiac monitor, making note of the baby's heart rate, which was higher than normal.

"Her lungs are clear," Dr. Ryan said in a low tone. "But she has hyperactive bowel sounds."

Cassie gave a nod. "Yes, she's also tachy, in the one-eighties. Dehydrated, perhaps?"

"Maybe," he agreed. "But could indicate something more serious. We don't have any history on the mother, unless we're lucky enough that the baby was born here.

Let's get her upstairs to the NNICU. She'll need an IV and labs drawn."

"Okay. I'll check the records when we get upstairs, but I don't think she was born here. I've been on the past three days and would have remembered." Cassie disconnected the electrical cord and switched the warmer to battery power. "Ready? Let's go."

Dr. Ryan walked along on the opposite side of the warmer. Cassie steered the warmer while he kept a keen eye on Emma's heart rate.

The elevator seemed to take longer this time, or maybe she was just acutely aware of Dr. Ryan standing next to her while listening to Emma's high-pitched crying. Her maternal instincts wanted her to pick the baby up and cradle her to her chest, but that wasn't possible just yet. When the elevator doors finally opened, she pushed the warmer inside with a sense of relief.

The doors closed and the elevator began rising to the third floor when Emma's high-pitched cries abruptly trailed off and stopped. Cassie stared in shock as the heart monitor began triple-beeping in alarm as the baby's heart rate shot up to two hundred beats per minute.

"She's not breathing," Cassie said, grabbing the emergency airway kit.

"Hand me the Ambu bag, I'll try to support her that way," he said.

She nodded, handing over the tiny Ambu bag and then connecting it to the oxygen tank. Her gaze darted between the heart monitor and Emma as he pressed the bag over Emma's nose and mouth, giving several breaths.

"It's working," she whispered. "Her heart rate is dropping back to the one-eighties."

"Good." Dr. Ryan's intense gaze met hers and for a moment she saw a flash of relief and camaraderie reflected there.

She tore her gaze away to glance down at the baby. "Poor thing doesn't have anyone to care about her," she murmured.

"She has us," Dr. Ryan said firmly. "We care about her. And we're going to do everything possible to help her."

She caught her breath at the emotion shimmering in Dr. Ryan's eyes but the moment vanished as the elevator door opened on the third floor. She pushed the warmer down the hall slowly enough to allow Dr. Ryan the ability to walk alongside while providing breathing support for the baby.

When they entered the NNICU, Cassie headed toward the critical-care end of the twenty-bed nursery, knowing that it was possible Emma would eventually require ventilator support for her breathing.

"Cassandra, I hear you're the best, so will you please start an IV?" Dr. Ryan asked as soon as they were situated.

"Of course." Getting IVs placed in babies wasn't easy, but it happened to be one of her best skills. The other nurses often asked her to start their IVs for them, so it shouldn't have surprised her that Dr. Ryan was aware of her talent. She could feel her cheeks getting warm and tried to keep her head down as she gathered supplies.

She managed to find a vein in Emma's left arm and quickly placed the catheter. Unfortunately, peripheral

IVs generally didn't last long in babies, twenty-four hours at the most, so the poor thing would likely need a new catheter placed tomorrow.

"What rate do you want the fluids to run at?" she asked, as she protected the catheter site with a plastic medicine cup cut in half and taped over the baby's arm so Emma couldn't dislodge it by accident.

"You have the IV placed already?" Dr. Ryan asked in surprise. "Good job. Let's start with five ccs per hour for now."

Cassie nodded and turned away to adjust the IV pump in an effort to hide her flaming cheeks. Ridiculous to respond like a high school cheerleader working with the star quarterback of the football team. It wasn't as if Dr. Ryan had given her a personal compliment.

In fact, the nurses all talked about how nice it was to work with him, despite the fact that he kept an invisible but impermeable wall between himself and the rest of the staff. She'd heard a few of the nurses had tried to ask him out, only to be gently but firmly rebuffed.

Her hormones needed to get a grip on reality.

"Let's see if she'll breathe on her own now," Dr. Ryan murmured, as he removed the Ambu bag and face mask from Emma.

Cassie leaned forward, watching the baby closely for a few minutes. She was just about to turn away when things changed abruptly, just like they had in the elevator. Emma's breathing became shallow and her pulse skyrocketed.

"Give her a tenth of a milligram of midazolam," Dr. Ryan ordered in a grim tone. "I need to intubate."

"I'll get the meds," her coworker, Diane, piped up.

Cassie pulled out the intubation equipment while Dr.

Ryan continued to breathe for Emma using the Ambu bag. When Diane returned a few minutes later, she held up the syringe for Cassie to verify the dose of the medication before injecting it into Emma's IV.

"Midazolam is in," Diane announced.

Cassie handed Dr. Ryan the tiny endotracheal tube. She found herself holding her breath, his words from the elevator echoing in her mind.

She has us. We care about her.

Soon Dr. Ryan had deftly placed the breathing tube down Emma's airway, a task that sounded simple but wasn't at all, not when working on a newborn baby. His large and capable fingers were never clumsy.

The entire procedure didn't take more than a few minutes and Cassie quickly secured the tube in place while Dr. Ryan held it steady. Nancy Kramer, the respiratory therapist, was manning the ventilator. "What settings do you want?" she asked.

He rattled off the parameters he wanted then turned toward Cassie. "I need you to get a set of arterial blood gases and a full drug screen."

"A drug screen?" Cassie glanced at what she could see of Emma's tiny face, half-covered with the endotracheal tube holder. "You think her mother was a drug addict?"

"Yes, I hate to say it, but I have a strong suspicion. The mother dropped the baby off in the ER, saying she wasn't a fit mother for Emma, and then left. Under the safe-haven law, we can't go after the mother to obtain a medical history, so we have to figure out what's going on ourselves. That high-pitched crying and the way she stopped breathing is a classic sign of narcotic

withdrawal. We'll also need to keep an eye out for seizures. Run the lab work and call me with the results."

Cassie nodded, feeling sick to her stomach. She had
to admit Emma's high-pitched cry did sound similar
to those of the two other babies she'd cared for early in
her career who'd been going through withdrawal. And
the timing was right, too. No doubt the baby's mother
hadn't been able to stand the baby's constant crying,
which had likely gotten worse over the hours since the
baby's birth.

She'd asked Alice to go through the records to see if
Emma had been born at their hospital, but soon discovered she was right, there was no record that matched
this baby. So where had Emma's mother given birth?
At home? Was she a resident of Cedar Bluff?

Even though Cassie had only worked at Cedar Bluff
Hospital for the past six months she knew a safe-haven
baby was a rare occurrence. Obviously they did get
them, but not often.

She was glad Emma's mother had been unselfish
enough to give up her baby, rather than neglect her or,
worse, hurt the child.

Still, it wasn't easy to see how some mothers would
easily give their babies away, when others, like herself,
had been unable to carry one to term.

A loss that still left an empty feeling inside her.

Ryan strode out of the NNICU, a dull roaring echoing
in his ears.

He knew the baby's blood tests would turn out positive for opiates. Thankfully he hadn't cared for drug-
addicted babies often, but the few times he had were
seared into his memory.

But worst of all, Emma was a painful reminder of the fact that if his son had lived, he would have made that same, high-pitched cry. Would have been born addicted to narcotics and would have suffered the same symptoms of opiate withdrawal.

At least Emma had been given a chance to survive. And, hopefully, thrive.

A chance his son hadn't been given.

He pinched the bridge of his nose with his fingers, trying to freeze out the horrible memories and the deep stabbing guilt. Three years had passed, yet the image of Victoria's pale, cold, lifeless face still haunted him.

He should have known. Somehow he should have known his wife had been addicted to painkillers. How had he missed the signs? Had he really been that blind to what had been going on?

Why hadn't he figured out the truth before it was too late? Before he'd found his wife and unborn son dead in the front seat of her car?

His fault. His son's premature death was his fault.

The elevator doors opened, and he pulled himself together, trying to remember where he was going. Oh, yeah, back to the ER. He doubted anyone would remember more than what he'd already been told but he felt compelled to ask.

The triage nurse—what was her name, Gloria?—was still sitting where he'd left her. "What do you remember about the mother?" he asked bluntly.

Gloria didn't seem too surprised by his question. "She had stringy blond hair and was young, not a teenager, maybe early to midtwenties? Her skin was super pale, as if she never stepped outside into the sun. And she wore long sleeves. Her arms shaking as if the car seat was too heavy for her."

Definitely drugs, he thought with a sigh. "Did she look at all familiar?"

"Not to me or anyone else who caught a glimpse of her. But I bet once the word gets out someone will come forward. Everyone knows everyone else's business in this town."

He nodded, knowing she spoke the truth. "Have the police been notified?"

Gloria thought for a minute. "I don't think so, to be honest. All I could think of was to get the NNICU team down here as quickly as possible. The way the baby was crying scared me."

He couldn't fault Gloria's logic. "All right, I'll give them a call." Emma's mother couldn't get into trouble for dropping off her baby at the hospital, but he figured the police should know about the possible drug connection.

And they'd have to get social services involved to find placement for the baby, too.

He walked to his office, seeking privacy to make his calls. First he notified the social worker on duty, who readily agreed to begin working on a temporary guardian and foster placement for Emma once she was stable enough for discharge. When he finished with that he debated between calling the police now or waiting until he had the actual test results.

A glance at his watch confirmed it was too late to get the drug-test results today as it was already five-thirty in the evening and drug tests were specialized enough that they couldn't be run on a stat basis. They'd be available in the morning, but he didn't want to wait that long to call the police. The sooner they knew about the issue, the better.

He dialed the sheriff's department, knowing the number by heart, and requested to be put through to a detective.

"This is Detective Trammel. What seems to be the problem?"

Of course Trammel would be the one on duty. Trammel had been the detective assigned to investigate Victoria's death. Ryan tightened his grip on the phone and tried to keep his voice steady. "This is Dr. Murphy at Cedar Bluff Hospital. I need to report we have a safe-haven baby here," Ryan informed him. "She was dropped off a little over an hour ago by a young woman with blond hair, roughly in her midtwenties."

"Dr. Murphy?" Detective Trammel echoed. "Dr. Ryan Murphy?"

"Yes." He knew that he wasn't a suspect any longer, but that first month after Victoria's death he'd been at the top of Trammel's list. Logically he understood that the police had wanted to rule out foul play, but it hadn't been easy to hold his head up within their small, tight-knit community.

Even three years later, it wasn't easy. But he hadn't wanted to leave, not until he'd uncovered the truth about the source of Victoria's drugs. He'd almost given up hope. Until now.

"How are you doing?" Detective Trammel asked, as if they were old friends. But they weren't. Not by a long shot.

"Fine," he said in a clipped tone. "You should know that I've already contacted the social worker, who's getting Child Protective Services involved."

"Okay, thanks. Wow, a safe-haven baby. We haven't had one of those in almost four years."

Ryan battled a wave of annoyance. This wasn't exactly a social call. "You need to know that I suspect the baby is addicted to drugs," he said bluntly. "We're running tests now."

A heavy silence hung between them and he imagined Detective Trammel finally figuring out why Ryan had bothered to make the call personally. "Okay, thanks for letting me know," the detective said finally. "But it's tricky to go after the mother in these situations. The safe-haven law offers protection, although there is wiggle room in cases of abuse."

"I'm well aware of the law," he said in a terse tone. "And I don't want to go after the mother per se. But what if we find that the baby was addicted to prescription narcotics? Don't you think that's something to be concerned about? Shouldn't we look for her supplier?"

"Your drug tests can't give that level of detail," Trammel protested.

He reined in his temper with an effort. "No, but the state lab in Madison could."

Another long silence. "Dr. Murphy, I told you before that we investigated the prescription-drug angle after your wife's death. There's no evidence of a prescription drug ring operating here in Cedar Bluff. Trust me, I'd know if there were."

Ryan felt his shoulders sag in defeat. He didn't believe the detective, yet there was nothing he could say that would change his mind, either. Because he didn't have proof.

Just a gut-level certainty he was right.

"Listen, Dr. Murphy, it's been almost three years

and I know it's difficult, but you need to move on with your life."

For an instant the image of Cassie's heart-shaped face, long chocolate-brown hair and warm brown eyes flashed in his mind. But he impatiently shoved it away.

"Let me know if the mother comes forward for some reason," he said to Detective Trammel, changing the subject. "Having some sort of medical history would be helpful."

"I will."

Ryan hung up the phone and sat back in his chair with a weary sigh. The detective was wrong—he *had* moved on with his life. He worked, and played softball in the summer and basketball in the winter with several other physicians on staff. So what if he avoided going out with women? He'd tried about a year or so ago, but the entire event had been a disaster. He'd wanted no-strings sex, but apparently that wasn't what Shana had wanted, despite the fact she'd assured him she did.

Even worse, the debacle had spread throughout Cedar Bluff Hospital. Staff whispering behind his back had only reminded him of that terrible time after Victoria's death.

No, getting tangled up with a woman wasn't part of his plan. No matter how tempted he might be, at least when it came to Cassie. And she was doubly off limits, since they worked together.

No, he had to remain focused on the issues at hand. He wished Detective Trammel had found some evidence of a prescription-drug ring in Cedar Bluff.

Because he wouldn't mind sharing a bit of the guilt that still weighed heavily on his shoulders over the deaths of his wife and unborn son.

CHAPTER TWO

CASSIE HOVERED OVER Emma's warmer, lightly stroking the tip of her finger down the baby's downy soft cheek, as much as she could around the breathing-tube holder.

Emma F. Safe Haven, the name they'd given her, was doing a great job of hanging in there. No sign of seizures yet, but Cassie was afraid that if she took her eye off the baby for an instant she'd miss the telltale jerky movements.

The good news so far was that Emma's blood gases had come back well within normal range. She'd placed a page in to Dr. Ryan to share the results. Maybe they could work on weaning the baby off the ventilator. They'd have to go slowly, because removing the tube, only to replace it a few hours later, would be traumatic and possibly cause damage to Emma's tiny airway. However, getting the baby off the vent was also better for Emma's lungs in the long run.

Finding the right balance was always tricky.

Cassie lingered a few minutes longer, wishing she could give Emma more of her attention, but then had to leave to care for the other baby assigned to her care. Thankfully Barton was stable. He'd been born four weeks too early, but was gaining weight and coming along nicely. He still had a couple instances of five seconds or longer of apnea, a common problem in preemies, but so far he'd gone twelve hours without any shallow breathing recorded on the monitor. If that trend continued, in another day or two he'd be ready to move up to the level-two nursery. And soon be discharged home.

She quickly changed Barton's soiled diaper and then disconnected him from the heart monitor for his feeding. She sank into a rocker she'd pulled over near Emma's warmer so she could keep an eye on Emma while giving Barton his bottle. Normally they encouraged the parents to come in for the feedings, but Barton's mother had mentioned she might be later than normal today because she had to wait for her husband to get home from being out of town. She'd had an emergency C-section and hadn't been cleared to drive yet.

"Aren't you a good boy," she cooed, as Barton eagerly sucked at his bottle. "You're going to grow up to be big and strong, just like your daddy."

She sensed someone's gaze on her and looked up to find Dr. Ryan standing a few feet away, staring at her. For a second she thought she saw a distinctive longing reflected in his eyes, but in a flash the moment was gone and the polite yet distant expression had returned to his eyes.

"Emma's blood gases look great, and I've entered new orders to drop her ventilator settings," he said brusquely. "Should I ask the unit clerk to page the respiratory therapist?"

"I'd appreciate that, if you don't mind. I'll be here for a while yet." More proof that Dr. Ryan was a great doctor. He didn't think menial tasks were beneath him.

Or maybe he was simply anxious to get Emma's vent settings changed. "So far I haven't seen any evidence of seizures."

"Good. You'll probably get a call from Child Protective Services, I put them on notice about Emma."

"Oh, okay." Cassie suppressed a flash of disappointment. Of course calling CPS was the right thing to do. "I guess, once she's stable, Emma will end up in foster care, then," she murmured, trying to hide the wistfulness in her tone. She had no right to be so emotionally attached to Emma. The baby wasn't hers to love and to care for. Except here, at work.

Dr. Ryan's lips tightened in a grim line. "I imagine so."

She couldn't say anything past the lump of regret lodged in her throat. Ridiculous to think she could become a foster parent for Emma. For one thing, there was a long process, including classes to take, along with other hoops to jump through, before she'd be granted that privilege. Even then, she knew that a married couple would have a better shot of getting custody of Emma than a single parent such as her.

Barton turned his face away from the bottle, reminding her it was time for a burp. She lifted him up, turned him and placed him against her shoulder, rubbing her hand in soothing circles over his back. She couldn't resist brushing a kiss against his downy temple, enjoying the scent of baby shampoo that clung to his skin. He squirmed a bit and made gurgling noises before letting out a loud belch.

"Good boy," she praised him with a wide smile. Gently she turned the baby round so she could try to give him the rest of his bottle. He was still pretty tiny, less than five pounds, so he usually only took a small portion of his bottle at each feeding.

"You're a natural," Dr. Ryan said in a low tone.

The longing to have a baby of her own stabbed deeply, but she pushed it away with an effort. Her cheeks warmed and she cursed herself for responding to every little thing Dr. Ryan said. He had no way of knowing that she'd miscarried twice before her marriage had shattered into irreparable pieces. "Thanks."

Abruptly he turned and walked toward the unit clerk's desk. She overheard him requesting the respiratory therapist on duty to be paged for vent setting changes.

Little Barton took another ounce before thrusting the nipple out of his mouth, indicating he wasn't interested in any more. She mentally calculated the total, pleased that he'd taken a half-ounce more at this feeding.

As she returned Barton to his bassinet and cranked on the mobile that hung over his head, she noticed Dr. Ryan was standing over Emma's warmer. She assumed that he was checking the baby's vital signs but as she approached she noticed that her little pink knit hat was off and he was softly stroking his thumb over Emma's downy head, murmuring softly.

"You're going to be fine, pretty girl. You'll see."

His words made tears prick her eyes and she subtly wiped them away. Dr. Ryan had called her a natural, but right now she was thinking the same about him. He was gazing down at Emma as if the baby was important on a personal level, rather than just another patient.

She hesitated, wondering if she was intruding, but he must have sensed her presence. He glanced at her and gently tugged the pink knit cap over Emma's head. "Do you need to get in here?" he asked.

"Yes, I need to check her vitals again," she said, trying to deal with her bizarre reaction to him. "But I can wait until you're finished."

"No, go ahead," he said, stepping back to give her plenty of room.

She avoided his gaze and tucked the buds of her stethoscope into her ears, taking her time to listen to Emma's heart, lungs and abdomen. When she straightened and pulled off the stethoscope, she caught Dr. Ryan's intense gaze resting on her once again.

She grappled for something intelligent to say. "Everything sounds good, but her bowel sounds are still hyperactive."

"I know. I'm reluctant to begin feeding her until we know for sure she won't start having seizures," he said, answering her unspoken question. "But if things continue to go well, I'll insert a feeding tube for bolus feedings."

"Sounds like a plan," she agreed. Since he was still logged on to the computer, she gestured toward it. "Do you need the computer?"

"Not at all." He leaned over to log off with quick keystrokes and she caught a whiff of his woodsy aftershave, the heady scent wreaking havoc with her senses. He stepped back, giving her room to sit, but he was still far too close for comfort.

Cassie tried to concentrate on documenting Emma's assessment, but it wasn't easy. She made several spelling mistakes, requiring her to backspace several times to fix them.

Why wouldn't he leave? Was he reading her charting,

double-checking her work? Surely he had better things to do. Better places to be other than here.

Validating vital signs was easier, merely requiring a point and click, and she was nearly finished when she heard him say her name in that deep, husky voice of his.

"Cassandra."

She couldn't seem to untie her tongue enough to tell him he could call her Cassie. After all, he insisted everyone call him by his first name, even though most continued to use his formal title, too. She glanced up, only to find his gaze glued to Emma.

Immediately, she rose to her feet. "What's wrong?"

"Get me point two milligrams of midazolam and a half milligram of phenobarbital. Emma is having a seizure."

Cassie's heart plunged to the pit of her stomach as she rushed over to the medication dispensing machine to get the medication.

She dashed back to Emma's warmer, holding each of the syringes up for him to see. "Point two milligrams of midazolam," she said. "And a half milligram of phenobarb."

"Yes, that's correct."

She gently injected the medications into Emma's IV then watched the baby's heart rate on the monitor.

She couldn't prevent an overwhelming sense of dread. Seizures were a bad sign. If they continued, there was a chance that Emma might suffer permanent brain damage.

The little girl could even die.

She has us. We care about her.

Cassie strengthened her resolve to do everything possible to make sure Emma had the best chance to survive.

* * *

Ryan shoved his hands in the pockets of his lab coat, hating every moment of feeling helpless.

This poor baby might not make it to her first birthday, all because her mother hadn't sought help for her addiction.

Anger was useless, so he did his best to breathe it away, keeping an eye on his patient instead. The medication worked and, thankfully, Emma's jerky movements stopped.

"I'm going to order the phenobarb to be given every six hours," he told Cassie. "And an EEG, too."

Cassie looked as upset as he felt, obviously already growing attached to their safe-haven baby. The same way he was. That moment in the elevator, when Cassie had mentioned the baby didn't have anyone to care about her, had tugged at his heart.

In the three years since losing Victoria and his son, he'd been able to keep a certain emotional distance from his tiny patients. Easy enough to do, as most of the time the babies got better and went home with their parents and families.

But knowing Emma was alone in the world made him feel differently towards her. He knew he was becoming emotionally involved with their safe-haven baby. And not just because she was sick enough to require his focused attention.

Because almost from the first moment he'd seen her, the little girl had found a way to break through the barriers surrounding what Shana had described as his stone-cold heart.

"Oh, Emma," Cassie murmured, stroking the baby's

cheek. "You've got to fight this, sweetpea. We're going to help you fight this."

His heart squeezed at the tears shimmering in Cassie's eyes. From the first day she'd started working here—had it just been a few months ago?—he'd noticed her creamy skin, heart-shaped face, bright brown eyes and long dark hair that she always drew back in a pony-tail at work, not to mention her curvy figure, mostly hidden beneath her baggy scrubs. What man wouldn't?

Look, but don't touch. That was his motto. Especially since the Shana debacle.

Yet for some reason, seeing Cassie cooing over the babies, especially Emma, hit him right in the center of his solar plexus.

He was irresistibly drawn to her. Had been from the moment they'd begun to work together. Resisting her was becoming more and more difficult. Maybe because she was the complete opposite in every way from Vic-toria. He'd never told anyone his deepest fear, that Vic-toria wouldn't have made a very good mother. Not the way Cassie would. She clearly loved her tiny patients.

Victoria had loved being a doctor's wife. Had loved entertaining guests and spending his money. He wasn't sure how she'd managed to keep herself busy every day, working out at the gym and then lunching with her friends.

When she'd blown out her Achilles tendon after a spin class, he'd supported her through surgery, im-pressed at how determined she'd been to get back to her normal routine. Even after she discovered she was pregnant, she didn't cut back on her exercise regimen. In fact, he suspected she'd doubled it in an effort to avoid gaining too much weight.

He'd gone back through his memories of that time often, trying to identify the signs he'd missed. But he'd been busy at work, taking everything Victoria had told him at face value.

Never suspecting, until far too late, that she'd become addicted to the painkillers the orthopedic surgeon had initially prescribed.

He shook off the past and forced himself to focus on the present. Just because he was deeply attracted to Cassie, it didn't mean he had any intention of acting on it. She was young, full of life and could do better than a broken man like him. He didn't plan to ever have a family of his own. He didn't deserve a second chance.

Forcing himself to turn away, he went over to a different computer, far away from the one Cassie had been using, to enter the medication orders. When he'd finished, he sat down to scroll through his other patients' charts.

It took him a few minutes to realize he was stalling. Ridiculous to think about waiting around here until the end of Cassie's shift. Just because he was on call, it didn't mean he shouldn't take advantage of the downtime to get some rest.

But before he could leave, his pager went off, announcing a pending crash C-section.

Rest would have to wait. "We need an emergency warmer down in the OR," he said.

"I'm ready," Diane said, hurrying toward him with the equipment. He knew that Cassie was already tied up with Emma and Barton, so he wasn't surprised that Diana was the nurse up for the next admission.

He strode purposefully toward the door, managing to resist the urge to glance back once more at Cassie.

She and Emma would be fine.

A few minutes later he entered the OR, where a laboring mother was lying on the table, her eyes full of fear. "Save my baby," she pleaded as the anesthesiologist tried to cover her mouth and nose with an oxygen mask. "Save my baby!"

"She has a prolapsed umbilical cord," Dr. Eden Graves informed him. "We need to move fast."

"Understood," he agreed. "I'm ready as soon as you are."

Leaving Diane to prepare their equipment, he walked over to look at the fetal monitoring strip. There were several steep decelerations present, indicating severe fetal bradycardia. He noted that the sharp drop in the fetal pulse coincided with highest portion of the uterine contractions. Classic sign of a prolapsed umbilical cord.

"Tip her uterus so that the pressure isn't on her cervix," he instructed.

"I did, but you're right, we could use more blankets to prop beneath her bottom."

A couple of nurses came over to assist and soon the patient was ready. The anesthesiologist gave Eden the high sign and she quickly began the procedure.

The baby was removed from the uterus within five minutes, and the minute the cord was cut he quickly took the infant over to the warmer. The baby boy wasn't too limp and quickly pinked up as they worked on him.

When the baby let out a wail, there was a collective sigh of relief from everyone in the room.

"Let me know what the cord blood gases show," he said to the circulating nurse in the room. "Page me with the results."

"Okay."

He finished his assessment with Diane's help and then deemed the infant stable enough for transport up to the neonatal nursery. Even though the baby boy looked fine for the moment, he intended to watch the infant for a few hours upstairs.

It was a good feeling to save a baby's life. Even though deep down he knew that no matter how many he saved, he'd always mourn the one that mattered most.

The son he'd lost.

Cassie was thankful Emma didn't show any more signs of seizures and the EEG tech seemed to think the test looked relatively normal. Of course, they needed the neurologist to read the test to know for sure, but she decided to remain optimistic.

Barton's parents were here, holding their son, so she decided this was a good time to take a quick break.

"Sally, would you mind keeping an eye on Emma for a few minutes? I'd like to run down to the cafeteria to grab something to eat."

"Sure, that's fine. But we're expecting that new baby to arrive within the next thirty minutes so make it quick, okay?"

"I will." She'd perfected the art of eating fast, to minimize disrupting patient care.

Leaving the unit, she took the stairs down to the cafeteria level. The grill line was too long, so she went over to the salad bar to make herself a quick grilled-chicken salad and fill a large cup with ice water. The hardest thing about working second shift was the inability to fall asleep once she got home, and the last thing she needed was the added impact of caffeine zipping through her system.

She sat down at a small table near the back of the cafeteria and quickly dug into her salad. A few nurses greeted her, but none of them lingered. Obviously the whole hospital was busy, not just her neonatal unit.

She kept an eye on her watch as she ate, knowing she needed to return to the unit before Dr. Ryan brought over his latest patient.

With any luck he'd be busy with the new admission for a while, giving her some badly needed breathing space. She really didn't understand what her problem was around him. There were plenty of other single guys around. James Green, one of the ER doctors, had asked her out just last month.

Too bad she hadn't felt one iota of interest in him. She'd politely declined James's offer, refusing to feel bad at the dejected expression in his eyes.

Her divorce had only been final for a little over a year. Six months ago she'd moved to Cedar Bluff to start afresh. It was too soon to enter the dating scene.

So why was she always so keenly aware of Dr. Ryan Murphy?

No clue. She shook her head, scraping the bottom of her salad bowl to get the last bit, before wiping her mouth with a napkin and rising to her feet.

Ten minutes. *Not bad*, she mused as she headed back toward the elevators. Walking up three flights of stairs seemed daunting after she'd practically inhaled her meal, so she took an elevator up.

She got off the elevator on the third floor and headed down the east hallway toward the neonatal unit.

Cassie frowned when she saw an older woman, probably in her midsixties, leaning heavily on a cane near the doorway. It looked as if the woman was trying to peer through the small window to see inside the unit.

"Good evening. Can I help you with something?" Cassie asked.

The woman started badly, spinning around so quickly she almost lost her balance. Cassie darted forward to slide a supportive arm around the woman's waist.

"Easy there, I don't want you to fall," Cassie said. "Is there something you need? Are you waiting to go in to visit?"

"Oh, no. I'm not waiting to visit. I…um…" The woman seemed flustered and avoided her gaze. "I was visiting a friend and thought I'd come over to peek at the babies. I'm sorry, I didn't mean to break any rules."

Since the woman obviously felt bad, Cassie decided she wouldn't push it. "That's okay, but you can't go in there unless you're related to one of the babies. It's a locked unit to protect them from being taken."

"Oh, of course. I—I'm sorry. I have to go." The woman took a step and leaned on her cane, making her way back toward the elevators. Cassie waited a moment, watching her.

It wasn't until she was back at Emma's bedside that she realized the woman might have being trying to catch a glimpse of Emma. Surely the news of their safe-haven baby had already spread throughout the small town of Cedar Bluff.

She wished she'd asked the woman for her name. Had she been peeking into the unit out of pure curiosity?

Or because she knew Emma's mother?

CHAPTER THREE

RYAN KEPT A close eye on the newborn baby boy for the next hour, relieved when the umbilical-cord blood-gas results weren't as bad as he'd feared.

The infant seemed to be doing well, so he drifted over to where Cassie was working with Emma.

"How's Emma doing?" he asked.

"Good," she said with a tired smile. "I haven't seen any seizure activity since we started her on the medication."

"Glad to hear it." He forced himself to tear his gaze away from her to focus on the baby, although he was very much aware of Cassie's warm vanilla scent. "Isn't your shift ending soon?"

"In another hour," she agreed. "I was supposed to be off tomorrow, but one of the nurses called in sick, so I agreed to come back for the day shift. Gives me a good excuse to check up on Emma."

He wasn't surprised she'd agreed to come back in less than eight hours. Over the past few months he'd discovered Cassie was always jumping in to help cover shifts as needed.

Despite his attempts to keep his distance, he found himself curious about why she devoted so much time

and energy to her work. He sensed she was using work
as a distraction from not having a personal life, the
same way he was.

He told himself the similarities between them didn't
matter, since he wasn't interested in having a relationship.

"They should let you leave early," he said with a
frown. "You deserve to get some rest."

"I'll be fine," she said with a wave of her hand. "I've
doubled back before and it's not too bad."

He was hardly in a position to argue, since his job
required him to be on call often. Too often, according to Victoria, who'd accused him of staying late at
work on purpose. Had he? Looking back now, he had
to admit there may have been a kernel of truth to Victoria's accusations.

He thrust the useless guilt aside. "I'm going to get
some rest in the call room, but page me if you need
anything."

"We will. But don't worry, I promise we won't bother
you unless it's important."

For a moment he was taken aback by her statement.
Was she actually trying to protect him? The concept
was so foreign he could barely wrap his mind around it.
"Call me anytime," he corrected, before turning away.

The attending physicians' call room was located just
outside the neonatal intensive care unit, close enough
for emergency situations but with enough soundproof-
ing to be able to get some sleep.

Ryan kept his scrubs on as he stretched out on the
narrow bed, so that he could rush out in a hurry for an
emergency. He closed his eyes and took several deep
breaths in an effort to relax.

Unfortunately, Cassie's face, etched with the deeply caring expression he'd seen while feeding Barton, bloomed in his mind. He cursed under his breath, knowing that if he didn't find a way to pry her out of his mind, he'd never get any sleep.

Too bad Cassie wasn't the type to go for a nice sweaty bout of no-strings sex. Because unfortunately, since he'd destroyed his chance to have a family, that's all he had left to offer.

Cassie groaned when her alarm went off at the ungodly hour of six o'clock in the morning. It felt as if she'd barely fallen asleep, as she'd tossed and turned until well past midnight, her thoughts darting from Dr. Ryan to Emma and back again. With a heavy sigh she dragged herself out of bed and stumbled toward the shower.

The hot water helped wake her up, although she wouldn't be human until she'd downed her first cup of coffee. Since blow-drying her hair would take too long, she pulled it back into a ponytail and applied enough makeup to cover the dark circles beneath her eyes.

Volunteering to help out had seemed like a good idea at the time, but in the bright light of morning she couldn't help wondering what in the world she'd been thinking.

Caring for Emma. That's what she'd been thinking.

Staring at the empty coffeepot, she realized grimly that she hadn't turned it on last night before crawling into bed. Feeling a bit desperate, she decided to stop at the local corner coffee shop before heading to the hospital.

The place was far more crowded than she'd have expected this early on a Friday morning. Although maybe the tourist crowd liked to get an early start. There wasn't any drive-through service, not since someone had knocked over the post holding the intercom and speaker, so she took her place in line, hoping things would move quickly.

Of course, they didn't. She glanced at her watch for the third time, thinking she should give up gourmet coffee for the icky stuff they brewed at work, when a second line opened up. "I can help the next person?" a woman called out.

The woman in front of Cassie darted over and she followed, figuring it would be quicker. Another person came up behind her and tapped her on the shoulder.

"Hey, Cass, how are you?"

Cassie glanced over her shoulder to see Gloria, her friend from the ER, standing behind her. "Good. How are you?"

"Fine. How's our safe-haven baby?" Gloria asked in a low tone.

"Critical but stable," she replied, knowing that the privacy laws prevented them from discussing patients. Although small towns like Cedar Bluff had a hard time with the concept of privacy. Everyone liked to meddle in everyone else's business.

"Oh, I heard about that," the woman in front of her said, turning around with her large coffee in hand. "Everyone's trying to figure out who the mother is."

Cassie shrugged and edged around the woman so she could place her order. "Large mocha coffee, please." She glanced back at the nosy woman. "The mother has the right to be anonymous, so I doubt we'll ever find out who she was. Besides, she did a good thing, giving her baby a chance at a better life."

"Cassie's right." Gloria spoke up, flashing Cassie an apologetic smile. "We should be thankful. I'm sure someone will step forward to adopt the baby."

"I guess you're right," the woman said, looking resigned at the fact she wasn't getting any good information.

Cassie turned back to accept her coffee, wishing once again that she'd gone through the process of becoming a foster parent back when she'd first investigated the option. At the time she'd convinced herself the notion was a knee-jerk reaction to losing her baby and discovering her ex-husband's betrayal. But if she had at least started the process, she'd be in a better position to adopt little Emma herself.

Was she crazy to even think of that as an option? Probably. But for some reason the idea wouldn't go away.

Cassie took a bracing sip of her coffee and headed back out to her car. The drive to the hospital didn't take long and she was still early enough to beat the worst of the traffic.

She stood by the elevator, sipping her coffee and thinking about the gossip that was already floating around about their safe-haven baby. If the mother was still around, she sincerely hoped the poor girl didn't overhear people talking about her.

Several of her coworkers joined her at the elevator, although it was too early for idle chitchat. When the elevator stopped on the third floor, Cassie waited for the nurses closest to the door to get out first, before following suit.

As she stepped out of the elevator she caught a glimpse of an older woman with a cane entering the adjacent elevator. Was it the same woman who had been peering through the window of the door last evening? She tried to dart around her coworkers, but the action proved difficult, like a salmon swimming upstream. By the time she cleared the group, the elevator doors had closed.

She hesitated, wondering if she should take the stairs down to the lobby to verify it was the same woman from yesterday. But a glance at her watch made her grimace. There wasn't enough time, she needed to punch in for her shift or she'd be late.

Besides, selfishly, she wanted to be sure Emma was assigned as her patient. So she hurried toward the door and swiped her ID badge over the electronic eye so she could get in.

Still carrying her coffee, she entered the staff lounge, where they generally congregated to make out the day's assignments. After glancing up at the whiteboard, she relaxed. The charge nurse on duty had already listed her name as the nurse for both Emma and Barton.

She sipped her coffee, waiting for the rest of the assignments to be made. Should she call security? And report what? A suspicious woman in her early sixties who used a cane?

Yeah, right. She was being ridiculous. For all she knew, the woman getting into the elevator wasn't the same one as the day before. And even if it was, so what? She'd mentioned she was here, visiting a patient. There were other units on the third floor besides the neonatal nursery.

Cassie pushed the thought of the cane lady out of her mind. Once the assignments were pretty much completed, she set her coffee aside, grabbed her stethoscope from her locker and headed over to Emma's warmer.

Her step faltered when she realized Dr. Ryan was sitting at the computer, reading through the baby's progress notes.

You are not a slave to your hormones, she told herself sternly. *You need to get over him already!*

She forced herself to continue walking, even as she swept her gaze over the area, looking for Debra, the night-shift nurse, who needed to give her the update on how Emma was doing.

"Good morning, Cassandra."

She blushed, giving him a nod. "Good morning, Dr. Ryan, and, please, call me Cassie."

There, she'd finally managed to sound casual, as if he were any other physician on staff.

"Only if you call me Ryan. And as you have such a beautiful name, it's a shame to shorten it." For a moment she felt her jaw drop in shock and did her best to close her mouth so she didn't look like a gaping fish. She was relieved when he changed the subject. "Emma's doing well this morning. I think we'll try to wean her a bit from the vent."

Okay, patient care she could handle. She took a deep breath. "That sounds like a good plan. What about nutrition?"

"She hasn't had any seizures since we started the medication, so it's probably okay to begin feeding her. As soon as I finish my morning rounds I'll come back to insert a feeding tube. Maybe you could get the pump set up so everything is ready to go."

"Of course." She avoided his direct gaze, not trusting her ability to stay cool, calm and collected.

Had he really called her beautiful? No, he'd called her name beautiful. And that was completely different.

Wasn't it?

Of course it was.

She pulled out her stethoscope and warmed the diaphragm in the palm of her hand before leaning over to listen to Emma's heart, lungs and abdomen. As she went through her basic assessment she swore she could feel Dr. Ryan's piercing gaze on the back of her neck.

Just as she finished her assessment Debra came rushing over. "Sorry I'm late, had to finish feeding Barton."

"We can start at his bassinet," Cassie said, hoping her need to escape Dr. Ryan's overwhelming presence wasn't too obvious. "I don't mind."

"Okay." Debra led the way over to where Barton's bassinet was located and quickly logged onto the computer to pull up his flow sheet. "He's up to two and a half ounces per feeding and he gained three ounces. His weight this morning is four pounds twelve ounces."

"Awesome news," Cassie said with a smile. "What about his breathing? Any periods of apnea noted on the monitor?"

"None. He's been clear for twenty hours now." Debra beamed as if she were the proud mama. Actually, they all tended to take great satisfaction from watching their tiny patients' progress. "If he lasts until tomorrow morning, Dr. Ryan is going to move him over to the level-two nursery."

"Wonderful," Cassie agreed. "His parents are going to be thrilled."

"They won't be here until later this afternoon, but I'm sure they will be." Debra clicked through the rest of the assessment, including the amount of time he needed to be placed under the bili lights, along with the medication list.

When they finished with Barton they went back over to Emma's warmer. Cassie was relieved yet oddly disappointed that Dr. Ryan had left. They quickly reviewed Emma's vitals, her vent settings and her medication list before Debra left to head home.

About an hour later Emma's IV pump began beeping. Fearing the worst, she hurried over to shut off the pump and check the IV site.

Emma's little vein had blown earlier than she'd expected. She removed the catheter, feeling bad about the bruise that marred Emma's pink skin.

"I'm so sorry, sweetpea," she murmured. "Unfortunately, I'm going to have to put this IV back in."

As much as she detesting having to poke the baby, she knew it was for Emma's own good. The poor thing needed to get her medication to prevent seizures. She was especially anxious to get some tube feedings into the little baby. Emma had lost the three ounces Barton had gained.

This time, she chose the opposite arm for the IV. Tiny beads of sweat rolled down from her temples as she concentrated on finding the vein. For some reason, putting an IV in Emma was much more stressful than when she placed them in other patients. Thankfully she managed to thread the tiny catheter in and breathed out a sigh of relief.

"Nice job," Dr. Ryan said from behind her.

Somehow she managed not to jerk the needle out of Emma's arm, in spite of the fact that he'd sneaked up on her. Again.

Completely her fault. After all, he had mentioned coming back after rounds to insert the feeding tube.

"Thanks. Just give me a minute here," she murmured, using the same contraption that she'd used yesterday to cover the IV site from being accidentally pulled out.

When she'd finished she stepped back and stripped off her gloves, trying not to imagine that most of her makeup had been sweated away. One thing about working over infants in warmers, you were never cold, even in the winter. In the summer, like today, it was downright steamy.

Although worth the discomfort, since their tiny babies needed every bit of the warmth.

"Has the social worker been by?" Ryan asked as he set out the feeding-tube supplies.

"Yes. She informed me that someone from Child Protective Services would be here between nine and ten."

"That should give me enough time to get the feeding tube placed."

"The pump is here and the formula you've ordered is ready to go."

A smile tugged at the corner of his mouth and she stared, acutely aware of how his face softened, making him look lighter. Younger. Not as detached.

"I should have known you'd be ready," he said. "Okay, Emma, we're going to have to get this nasty tube in," he said in a soft voice as he leaned over the baby. He lightly ran his finger down the length of Emma's arm and she was struck by the fact that this was the second time he'd soothed Emma, something she hadn't seen him do to any of the other babies in their care.

"But, trust me, you'll feel better with some food in your tummy."

Just like the IV, a feeding tube was a necessity for babies on ventilators. Even without the breathing support, Emma would likely need to be tube fed because of the seizure medication.

She helped hold Emma's head and body steady as Dr. Ryan inserted the feeding tube. Emma didn't like it much. Her tiny arms and legs flailed a bit, but then the tube was in her stomach and the worst of the discomfort was over.

"I'm so glad she won't remember this," Cassie murmured. "I feel like we're torturing her."

"We're not," Dr. Ryan said softly. "She's strong, she'll pull through this."

"I know," she said huskily, trying not to give in to the urge to cry. No baby should have to suffer and it was hard not to pass judgment on the baby's mother for allowing this to happen.

She subtly swiped at her eyes and turned to the feeding pump to program in the proper rate. Ryan came up beside her and put his hand lightly on her arm.

"Are you all right?" he asked in a husky voice.

She wasn't, but partially because his skin was so warm and tingly, she couldn't think. "Um, sure. I'm fine. Emma's the one I'm worried about."

"Me, too. But I'm confident you'll take good care of her. You're an incredible nurse, Cassie," he murmured.

"I'm not," she protested. "I just happen to love babies."

"I can tell. As I said before, you're a natural."

She glanced up at him, mesmerized by his ocean-blue gaze. Awareness shimmered between them, and suddenly she couldn't seem to remember why she needed to keep her distance from him. He seemed to understand her so well.

Better than her husband ever had.

With an effort, she tore her gaze away to glance back down at Emma. She knew very well why she needed to stay away. She'd suffered two miscarriages and her doctor had told her not to get pregnant until she'd had surgery. And even then, he'd told her, there could be scarring, preventing her from ever having a baby of her own.

And deep down she was afraid to risk getting pregnant again. She might not survive the emotional distress of another miscarriage.

"Cassie?" Ryan's voice pulled her from her sad thoughts. But before he could say anything more, the social worker approached, accompanied by a woman in her midforties wearing a badly fitting suit.

"Hi, Cassie, Dr. Murphy. This is Judith from CPS."

Cassie stepped away from Ryan and nodded at Judith. "Good morning."

"Good morning. What can you tell me about Emma's condition?" Judith asked, getting right down to business. The way she barely glanced at the baby grated on Cassie's nerves.

"She's been a sick little girl, but she's stable at the moment. We're supporting her breathing and giving anti-seizure medication."

"I see. What's the cause of her illness?"

"Her lab tests just came back positive for opiates, although the level isn't as high as I expected," Ryan admitted.

"So the mother was a drug addict." Judith didn't

look at all happy with the news. "We could go after the mother for child abuse."

"Please, don't." Cassie spoke up. "She gave up her child under the safe-haven law. If the word gets out that we're going after the mother, others may not risk doing the same."

Judith grimaced and nodded. "I know, but it still makes me angry. How long before the baby is able to be discharged?"

"I can't tell you for sure, but probably a week or two, maybe more. Depends on how well she responds to treatment."

"Do you have foster care lined up yet?" Cassie asked.

"No. Actually, the fact that she's likely going through withdrawal and will probably have ongoing medical issues makes placement more difficult." Judith scowled, as if Emma had done it on purpose.

"Why is that?" Cassie demanded. "What difference does it make if she has medical needs?"

Judith shrugged. "Many people aren't willing to take on that kind of commitment," she said.

"I will," Cassie blurted, without stopping to think. "I'll go through the process of becoming a foster parent and I'd be more than willing to take Emma home with me. No matter what her medical issues are."

Judith and Ryan stared at her as if she'd lost her mind, but now that she'd said it out loud, she knew she'd meant every word.

She couldn't help thinking that this was meant to be. That she was meant to be Emma's mother.

And she knew she'd love Emma as her own child, if given the chance.

CHAPTER FOUR

RYAN WAS STUNNED to hear Cassie blurt out how much she wanted to be a foster parent for Emma, although truthfully, he shouldn't have been. Her gaze was bright with compassion and from the way she cared for their tiny patients, he knew she'd make an excellent mother. In fact, he was surprised she hadn't already been snatched up by some lucky guy.

Just the mere idea of Cassie being with anyone else was repugnant, and he clenched his jaw, trying to hide his reaction. Certainly she wouldn't blush the way she did every time he spoke to her if she was seeing someone else.

Would she?

"Have you applied to be a foster parent?" Judith asked, staring at Cassie expectantly.

"No, but I'm happy to do that," Cassie said without hesitation. "I finish my shift today at three-thirty. I can be at city hall before four."

Judith's expression wasn't encouraging. "If you haven't started the process, then you likely won't be approved in time to take care of Emma."

Ryan felt compelled to butt in. "Is there anything Cassie could do to expedite the process? If placing

Emma will be as difficult as you say, this would be a win-win situation for both of them."

Cassie's gaze met his, full of silent gratitude. "I'll do whatever you ask, provide whatever you need," she said to Judith. "I'll take days off work if I have to."

"There's no way I know of to get through the process any sooner, but you can certainly ask about that when you go to city hall." Judith obviously considered the matter closed as she turned back toward Ryan and the social worker. "I'll return to check on the baby early next week. If anything changes in the meantime, either for the better or for the worse, I'd appreciate a call."

"Of course," he agreed. Even though he didn't particularly like the case worker, he knew that they needed to try to stay on Judith's good side if at all possible. Especially if Cassie was really going to go through with the plan of becoming a foster parent, an idea he was still trying to wrap his mind around. "Is there anything else you need from us?"

"Not right now." Judith glanced at them and shrugged. "Have a good day."

"You, too," Cassie said, with a forced smile.

He waited until the social worker had escorted Judith out of the unit before turning toward Cassie. "Do you really think this is a good idea?" he asked.

"Yes, I do," she answered without hesitation. "I know it seems like a snap decision, but it's not."

Ryan wasn't sure why he kept pressing the issue. "I know you love babies, but don't you think that having a child as a single parent will be difficult? Not to mention putting a crimp in your social life?"

She squared her shoulders and lifted her chin stubbornly. "I don't have a social life. After my ex cheated on me, I'm not anxious to trust men enough to try the dating scene again. I know being a single mother won't be easy, but I'm determined to provide Emma with a loving home. And as a nurse I can help with any medical issues she might have. Maybe Judith is right and I'm too late, but I still plan to move forward, hoping for the best."

He wanted to tell her that her ex-husband was a jerk to sleep around on her, but hadn't he let Victoria down, too? Maybe he hadn't cheated on Victoria but he hadn't been there for her. Still, he deeply admired Cassie's willingness to put her needs on the back burner in order to provide a home for Emma. "I'll be willing to provide you a reference if needed," he offered.

"Really?" The way her entire face lit up with hope and happiness made his pulse jump erratically. She'd never looked more beautiful to him than she did in that moment. She literally took his breath away. "Thank you so much, Dr. Ryan! You have no idea how much that means to me."

He struggled to come up with a reasonable response when he could barely think straight. "No problem. And if you need help with the paperwork, let me know."

"Oh, I'm sure I'll figure it out," she assured him.

He hesitated, loath to leave, even though he knew his colleague, Matthew Marks, would be there soon to relieve him. Matt should have been there already, but had asked for a couple extra hours off.

"Is there anything else you need, Dr. Ryan?" she asked, when she noticed him still standing there.

Irrationally, he wished she'd call him by his first name, the way he'd asked her to. Ryan knew it was better to keep things on a professional level, but he still yearned for her to address him as more than a colleague. He shook off his ridiculous thought. "No, just make sure you document how well Emma tolerates her feedings. I'm leaving as soon as I sign off with Dr. Marks, but I'll check her chart later this afternoon."

"Okay. She's going to do great, I'm sure." She turned and stroked Emma's cheek, the way he'd seen her do many times before. "Hang in there, sweetpea. We're going to give you some food to help you grow big and strong. You're going to be just fine, you'll see."

The way Cassie soothed Emma made him wish desperately that things could be different. He'd been fighting the chemistry sizzling between them for a couple of months now, knowing he couldn't dare act on it. Not just because they worked together, although that certainly didn't help matters, but because she deserved someone better than him.

Finding Victoria and his unborn son dead from an accidental overdose had broken something deep inside him. A portion of his heart that he didn't have a clue how to fix.

As much as he adored children, he wasn't ready for a relationship. Not now.

Maybe not ever.

Cassie glanced over her shoulder, watching covertly as Ryan walked away. That had been the most personal conversation they'd ever had and she couldn't imagine why she'd told him about her ex. And then he'd shocked her further when he'd jumped to her defense with the case worker from Child Protective Services. Maybe he had reservations about her idea of applying to be a foster parent for Emma, but that hadn't stopped him from offering to give her a reference.

She knew she shouldn't read too much into his actions, although at the same time she was certain she hadn't imagined the spark of attraction that had sizzled between them.

The very idea that he might be as attracted to her as she was to him made her face go hot. And she couldn't deny a tiny sense of panic. How could she go out with someone as amazing as Ryan? Her ex had been a handsome pharmacist, with women throwing themselves at him, and she hadn't been enough to satisfy him. Plus, Ryan didn't know the truth about her miscarriages, either.

She took deep breaths to calm herself down. Most likely Ryan was just being nice. He obviously cared about Emma's fate. And she was exhausted from her restless night. Maybe she'd imagined the awareness between them. Imagined the husky way he'd said her full name.

Cassandra.

Her knees went weak and she dropped into the seat near Emma's computer. What was wrong with her? This wasn't the time or place to think about the attraction she felt for Ryan. She needed to keep her mind focused on important matters, like giving Emma her first tube feeding and placing eye protection on Barton prior to placing him beneath the bili lights.

But as she cared for little Barton, Ryan's voice lingered in her mind. When the baby's parents came in to give him his noon feeding, she was grateful to head over to spend more time with Emma.

The baby's seizure precautions were still in place,

despite the fact that there hadn't been any documented seizure activity since the first one shortly after her admission. Still, Cassie knew they needed to be careful not to overstimulate Emma. Too much stimulation could actually cause the seizures to return. So after giving Emma her second feeding Cassie settled behind the computer to look up information on being a foster parent.

The amount of paperwork was overwhelming, but she refused to let that stop her. She printed out the application and the instructions, tucking them in her purse so she could review the information on her break.

Her shift dragged by slowly, no doubt because she was anxious to get to city hall. The fact that Ryan had gone home, leaving Dr. Matthew as the neonatal intensivist in charge, had nothing to do with it.

At least, that's what she tried to tell herself. Not very convincingly either.

To keep Ryan from crowding her thoughts, she focused on getting all her work finished. By two forty-five, Cassie was ready to go. She went over one last time to Emma's warmer, realizing that as she was off on Saturday, she wouldn't get to see the baby until her shift started on Sunday at three o'clock in the afternoon.

"You're doing so well, sweetpea," Cassie murmured, stroking the baby's downy cheek. "I'm sorry I won't see you for a day and a half, but I'll be thinking of you."

She gently checked Emma's IV in her arm and stroked the tip of her finger down her forearm to her hand. The baby caught her off guard by grabbing hold of her index finger in a surprisingly tight grip.

"That's my girl," Cassie said, tears pricking her eyelids. "You're getting stronger already, aren't you?"

Emma clung to her finger for a long minute before letting go and Cassie found herself wishing Ryan were here to share the thrilling moment. With babies you had to measure success in small increments. Emma had kept down the two bolus feedings and had grasped her finger. Huge accomplishments for a three-day-old baby born addicted to narcotics.

Sheri, the second shift nurse, came over at ten minutes after three and Cassie quickly went through Emma's orders with her. They double-checked Emma's IV site and the pump settings together before crossing over to Barton's bassinet. Sheri was familiar with Barton's care as he'd been with them for a week already, so going through his orders didn't take long.

Since Sheri had everything under control with Emma and Barton, Cassie swiped out of work fifteen minutes early, anxious to head straight out to her car. She was so focused on her mission that she didn't hear her friend Gloria, who was leaving at the same time, call out to her.

"Cass? Wait up a minute," Gloria said in a loud voice, sounding a tad annoyed.

"I'm sorry, I didn't mean to be rude," Cassie apologized. "I'm just in a hurry." Cassie slowed down so Gloria could catch up. She tried not to glance at her watch, which would only broadcast her impatience.

"Ooh, does that mean you have a hot date?" Gloria teased.

Ryan's face involuntarily flashed in her mind, even as she let out a sigh. "Don't be silly, of course not."

"Listen, Cass, I know your ex was a jerk, betraying you in the worst way possible, but locking yourself away from all men isn't the answer. James was upset that you turned down his offer to take you out for dinner, but I'm sure he'd give you a second chance."

Oh, boy. She *so* did not want to have this conversation, especially now. Obviously Gloria was trying to help, but there was no way Cassie was going to confess feelings for Ryan that she didn't even understand herself. Dating anyone else was out of the question.

"Listen, Gloria, I'm not locking myself away from men. I can't help the fact I'm not the least bit attracted to James. Please, don't try to set me up with anyone else, either. I'll find someone on my own when the time is right for me. Besides, I'm really running late, so let's chat later, okay?" Without waiting for Gloria to respond, she quickened her step, using her key fob to unlock her car.

"Call me," Gloria shouted as she slid behind the wheel.

Cassie quickly started her car and opened the windows to let the stuffy air out. "I will," she called back, before putting the vehicle in Reverse and backing out of the parking space.

Cassie had to stop at her apartment to pick up a copy of her birth certificate and social security card. Since she was there, she decided to change out of her scrubs, donning a flowery skirt and short-sleeved top. Slipping her feet into comfy sandals, she headed back outside.

From her apartment, the drive to city hall didn't take long. Cedar Bluff was crowded with tourists in the summer, but even then there wasn't normally a rush-hour traffic problem.

She climbed out of her car and approached the building with all the paperwork clutched in her hand, struck by a feeling of trepidation. What if they immediately turned her down because she was single? What if they thought her apartment was too small to be an appropriate home for Emma? She planned on buying a small house, but needed to save some more money first.

"Cassandra, is something wrong?"

She jerked her head around at the sound of Ryan's voice. For a moment she blinked, wondering if she was losing it. But, no, there he was, sexier than ever, wearing casual jeans and a well-worn ocean-blue T-shirt that brightened his already mesmerizing blue eyes. And she was suddenly relieved she'd changed out of her scrubs.

Had he really come there just for her?

"Um, no. Of course not." She smiled, shoving her irrational doubts away. "But I'm surprised to see you. Is there something you need? Did I forget to document something in Emma's chart?"

The corner of his mouth kicked up in a wry smile. "No, you didn't forget anything. I'm thrilled she's doing so well." He hesitated and then shrugged. "It's always better if I keep busy the day after I'm on call, otherwise I'm not able to sleep at night. I thought I'd meet you here in case you needed help."

She was humbled by the idea that Ryan had come there for nothing more than to offer his support. Was it possible that little Emma had captured his heart, the same way she'd captured hers? She'd assumed that he didn't date because he didn't want a family. But after seeing the way he'd been with Emma, she knew that couldn't be right. "That's so nice of you."

For a moment their gazes clung and the air sizzled with tension, but then he turned his head and gestured to the paperwork in her hand. "Do you need to finish up any of that paperwork before we go inside?"

It took her a minute for the synapses in her brain to fire on all cylinders. "Oh, no, I have it completed," she assured him, pushing aside the temptation to have him go through everything as a double check. "But thanks."

"No problem."

The low timbre of his voice sent shivers down her spine, causing her to blush. Again. Seriously, she really needed to stop feeling like a young teenager around him. She'd been married, for heavens' sake. And divorced.

The memory was sobering. Could she really trust another man not to hurt her the way Evan had? Her stomach clenched. A handsome, aloof doctor was not the best candidate.

But somehow Ryan didn't seem as aloof around her.

"Are you ready?" Ryan asked, interrupting her tumultuous thoughts by placing his hand beneath her elbow.

"Of course." She pulled herself together with an effort, taking the necessary steps to reach the front door of the building. Before she could open the door, Ryan was reaching around her to open it for her.

If anything, her blush deepened. "Thanks," she said, entering the building and hoping the blessedly cool air-conditioning would help make the redness fade from her skin.

There were a couple of people ahead of her, so she took her place in line to wait her turn. Ryan stood right beside her, making her more conscious of his intimidating height and the breadth of his shoulders. Did he work out in a gym in his spare time? Feeling insecure, she sucked in her stomach, making a mental note to go for a run later that evening.

When it was her turn, she walked up to the counter and spread out her application, along with the documents she'd brought from home, for the woman to review.

But she was disappointed when the clerk simply gathered them together into a pile, without reading a word. "Thanks. We'll get this processed and be in touch."

Crestfallen, Cassie turned away, but Ryan didn't.

"Good afternoon. I'm Dr. Ryan Murphy from Cedar Bluff Hospital and Cassie needs to know if there is anything she can do to speed up the process of becoming a foster parent. There's a baby in my care that needs to be placed with her as soon as possible."

The woman's eyebrows shot up in surprise. "Um, I'm sorry, but I can't help you. I'm just a clerk. I take the paperwork and file it as instructed."

Cassie leaned forward, determined to stand up for herself, too. "Who is the person in charge, then? I need to talk to whoever that is."

"Mr. Davies is in charge of the Child Protective Services department, but I'm afraid you'll need an appointment."

"Fine. Will you please give me his contact information?" Cassie asked.

The flustered clerk took out a card and scribbled Mr. Davies's name and number on the back. "Here you go. He's probably already gone today, but I believe he'll be back in the office on Monday."

Cassie took the card and nodded. "Thank you." She turned and headed back outside, feeling foolish for having built her hopes up over nothing.

"Well, that was a bit anticlimactic," Cassie said with a wry smile. "But thanks for coming anyway, Dr.— er...Ryan."

Ryan's smile made her tummy flip-flop again. "Spending time with you is never anticlimactic," he assured her in his deep voice. "I want you to let me know if Mr. Davies doesn't get back to you. I'm willing to put on the heat if needed."

"Thanks, but I'll get through to him." Cassie was determined to get this accomplished on her own, even though it was nice to have Ryan cheering her on.

She was heading toward the parking lot when she caught a glimpse of the cane woman.

Her hand shot out to grasp Ryan's arm. "Do you see that woman with the gray hair, walking with a cane? The one wearing white slacks and a green blouse?"

"Yes, why?" Ryan asked with a frown.

"This is the third time I've seen her in the last two days," Cassie said, keeping her voice low so no one else could hear. "The first time I caught her peering in through the window of the neonatal unit."

"That's odd," Ryan agreed.

"It can't be a coincidence," Cassie murmured. "Although what is she doing here at city hall? She couldn't possibly have known I was coming. I only made that decision earlier today."

"I hope she's not following you," Ryan said with a scowl.

Cassie couldn't deny the thought of this woman following her was creepy. "Ryan, I think she knows something about Emma. I bet she knows Emma's mother. In fact, she might even be related to the baby in some way."

"There's only one way to find out," Ryan said. "We need to talk to her."

Cassie nodded. "I agree."

But when they skirted the parked cars to head over to the sidewalk, the woman wasn't anywhere in sight.

CHAPTER FIVE

RYAN COULDN'T BELIEVE the woman Cassie had pointed out to him had managed to disappear so quickly. "She must have gotten into a car and driven off," he muttered in disgust. "There's no way she could have walked that fast with a cane."

"You're right," Cassie agreed with a frown. "Too bad we didn't get a glimpse of the car, either."

"Do you think there's a chance she's faking the need for a cane?" he asked. "Maybe there's more sinister to this woman than we realize."

"No, I don't think so," Cassie argued. "I've seen her up close and she definitely isn't steady on her feet. In fact, she would have fallen down if I hadn't supported her. I'm sure she's harmless enough."

Ryan blew out a heavy breath. "Okay, then, there's nothing more we can do right now. We don't even know her name. Although I'd love to talk to her, especially if she really does know something about Emma. If we could validate the mother's medical history, we'd have a better chance of treating her."

"I know. Trust me, the next time I see her, I'll get her name," Cassie said. "She must be trying to find information about Emma, nothing else makes sense."

"Probably. Although I don't like the way she's latched onto you."

"I know," Cassie said with a grimace. "I mean, there are lots of neonatal intensive care nurses—why would she assume I'm the one who might know something about Emma?"

Ryan didn't like the idea of this woman following Cassie, even if she didn't pose a physical threat. He frowned, thinking back over the past two days. "Maybe she was in the ER when Emma's mother dropped her off," he theorized. "If she was there she would have seen us caring for Emma."

"Could be," she agreed. "Or if she was looking through the window of the neonatal unit for a while, she might have watched me taking care of Emma."

Cassie turned around to head back to her car, so Ryan fell into step beside her. The last thing he wanted to do was to go back to his empty house, which had actually never been a home. Too bad he hadn't figured that out until it had been too late.

He and Victoria had gotten married too young. Looking back, he knew he'd mistaken lust for love. But he'd tried to make their marriage work. Victoria's death proved he hadn't succeeded. More to feel guilty about. Had Victoria loved him in a way he hadn't been able to love her?

He shook his head to stop the endless round of useless questions. His steps slowed to a stop, and he knew he couldn't bear to spend the rest of the evening alone. And he hadn't been lying about his need to keep busy on his post-call day. Maybe Cassie was just the distraction he needed.

"Would you be willing to join me for dinner?" he asked.

She blinked, apparently caught off guard by his offer. "I don't know. From what I hear, you don't date nurses from the hospital."

He tried not to wince. "That's true. But this isn't a date, just two people sharing a friendly meal."

The way Cassie stared at him made him wonder if his nose was growing. Did she see right through his lie? And why was he breaking his cardinal rule now? After months of resisting her?

"I suppose sharing a friendly meal wouldn't hurt," she said, although the way she avoided his direct gaze made him realize he could have handled that better.

"Please," he added. "It's too nice to spend the evening indoors. And there's an outdoor café a few blocks from here." He wanted to rush her over there before she could change her mind.

Before he could change his mind.

He knew only too well the power of gossip. Once the citizens of Cedar Bluff saw them together, there would be no stopping the rumors. Just that thought alone should send him running in the opposite direction.

But he didn't move. For some reason, he didn't want to lose the tenuous connection he had with Cassie.

A connection that made him feel alive again.

"Do you think I can leave my car here?" She frowned, glancing around the mostly deserted parking lot. "Or will I get a ticket?"

"You can park here and I'll walk you back when we're finished," he promised. He rested his hand on the small of her back, guiding her toward the Sunshine Café, located just a couple of blocks down from city hall. He groaned inwardly when he noticed how crowded the place was, but fate seemed to be working in his favor because when they stepped up to the hostess stand, a couple vacated their seat on the patio.

"We'd like to sit outside, please," he said, gesturing to the now open table.

She smiled. "Of course. Follow me."

The hostess led them over to the empty table and he pulled out Cassie's chair for her, before taking the seat across from her.

"Maria, your server, will be with you shortly," the hostess said as she placed two menus on the table in front of them. "Enjoy your meal."

"This is nice," Cassie said, looking around in awe. "I haven't eaten here before."

"The food is excellent and they renovated this area last year to provide more patio seating."

"It's beautiful." She sat up, peering over his shoulder. "Ryan, look! We can see Lake Michigan from here."

He nodded, glancing over his shoulder and smiling at her enthusiasm. "Yes, the view is part of the charm. What would you like to drink?" he asked, when he noticed their server was headed in their direction. "Wine? Beer? Lemonade?"

"Oh, well, I'm not sure," she said, looking down at the menu. He loved the way she blushed, her pink cheeks making her even more adorable. "Actually, lemonade sounds great."

"Sounds good. We'll start off with two lemonades," he told the server.

"I'll get those for you right away," Maria assured them.

An awkward silence fell once they were left alone,

and Ryan tried to think of something to say that wouldn't sound like they were on a date.

"So tell me, were you busy last night?" she asked.

He glanced up in surprise, not at all accustomed to talking about his job. Victoria hadn't wanted to know about the situations he'd faced on a daily basis, claiming she couldn't bear to hear about sick babies. At the time he hadn't blamed her, but now having Cassie's interest focused on him made him realize how much he'd missed sharing the important work he did. "There was a delivery about three in the morning that was touch and go for a while. Thankfully the baby survived."

Cassie's gaze softened. "I'm so glad. Daniel, right? His warmer is located next to Emma's. Poor little guy is on a ventilator, too."

"Yes, that's right. He was pretty pale at first, but his mother was healthy, so I'm sure he'll do fine." He relaxed in his seat, savoring the moment. When had the last time been that he'd simply enjoyed being with someone? He honestly couldn't remember. "I shouldn't complain. I managed to get about four hours of sleep before I was needed to head down to the delivery, so it could have been worse."

"That's not much sleep at all," Cassie protested. "But I understand now why you want to stay up today. I used to do the same thing when I worked the night shift. It's not easy to get back on a normal sleep schedule, is it?"

"No, it's not," he admitted wryly.

Maria returned with their lemonades. After going through their specials, she left them alone to peruse the menu.

"The grilled chicken and almond salad looks delicious," Cassie said, as she reviewed the selections.

"I'm having the Swiss mushroom burger," he said. He knew from experience that most women worried too much about what they ate.

"Yeah, you had to point that out, didn't you?" she said with a groan. "The Swiss mushroom burger sounds delicious. To be honest, I'm really hungry. I skipped lunch so I could fill out the foster-care paperwork."

"You won't regret the burger," he promised, capturing her gaze with his. "And you shouldn't skip meals, it's not good for you."

She wrinkled her nose at him. "Trust me, I don't skip meals very often. Okay, you sold me on the Swiss mushroom burger." She closed her menu and set it aside.

Maria returned to take their order. He took a sip of his lemonade, liking the way Cassie looked, seated across from him.

"Tell me why you don't date nurses from the hospital," Cassie said, her tone deceptively casual.

He winced and set his glass down, surprised by the way she'd gotten straight to the point. "I tried that about a year ago, but things didn't work out."

"Hmm," she said, tipping her head to regard him thoughtfully. "I sense there's more to that story."

Ryan didn't want to admit that he'd been so callous as to want nothing more than sex. And since Cassie was new here, she might not know about his past.

A past that would haunt him forever.

But he couldn't bring himself to lie to her. "My wife died almost three years ago," he admitted, surprising himself with his willingness to talk about the past. "I wasn't ready for a serious relationship."

"Oh, Ryan." Cassie's expressive brown eyes filled

with empathy and she reached across the table to take his hand in hers. "I'm so sorry for your loss."

He felt like a total fraud and could barely force air past his tight throat. "Thanks. The circumstances were…difficult." He cleared his throat, unable to say anything more. He couldn't bear the thought of Cassie knowing all the gory details. "Enough about me. I need you to know how much I admire you for wanting to be a foster mother to Emma. Being a parent is the most important job in the world."

Her gaze clung to his for a long moment, as if she knew he was changing the subject on purpose. But then she released his hand and sat back in her seat.

"Thanks. But I'm not doing this to impress anyone," she said softly. "I bonded with Emma right from the beginning. I know it sounds illogical, especially since I've only known her for twenty-four hours, but she's very special to me."

"To me, too," Ryan admitted. He gazed into Cassie's passionate eyes, struck by the sweeping desire to kiss her, right here, right now. He curled his fingers into a fist to prevent himself from reaching out to her. Thankfully their server chose that moment to return.

"Are you ready to order?" she asked cheerfully.

Ryan forced himself to nod. He took a big gulp of his cold lemonade, trying to get himself under control.

"I'd love to try your Swiss mushroom burger," Cassie announced.

"What would you like for a side? French fries, home-made chips or coleslaw?" Maria asked.

Cassie hesitated then shrugged. "Chips. I can't resist homemade chips," she confessed.

"I'll have the same," he managed. "And another refill on the lemonade when you have a minute."

"Sure thing," Maria promised, gathering their menus.

Ryan stared at his soft drink, wishing now that he had asked for something stronger. Maybe if he dumped the ice over his hot head, he'd cool off faster. Normally he didn't have trouble controlling his basic desires.

But he was beginning to think that there was nothing normal about his growing feelings for Cassie.

And he was damned if he knew what to do about that fact.

Cassie enjoyed every bite of the diabolically delicious Swiss mushroom burger, making a mental note to double the length of her planned run. The homemade chips were awesome, too, and she had to stop herself from eating them all, tossing her napkin over her plate to hide them from view, even though she knew Evan wasn't here to give her a hard time about what she ate.

Ironically, Ryan didn't seem to mind her hearty appetite. The way he kept staring at her with that intense gaze of his was a bit intimidating. She wasn't used to being the center of any man's attention. Especially a guy like Ryan.

Her heart ached for him. Losing his wife couldn't have been easy. No wonder he didn't date the nursing staff. She could easily imagine some nurse thinking she'd make the next Mrs. Ryan Murphy.

All the more reason to get any thoughts of being with him right out of her head. She had enough personal issues of her own to deal with, including becoming a foster mother to Emma.

Still, she couldn't help noticing just how different

Ryan was from her ex-husband. Evan had never gazed at her so intently. In fact, he'd often stared at other women, even when she'd been sitting right there. Several times since the divorce, she'd wondered why she'd thought she'd loved Evan in the first place. It hurt to realize she may have been looking for the security of marriage rather than being truly in love. And she wished she'd figured that out sooner.

Before she'd lost her second baby.

She didn't want to ruin the moment by dwelling on the mistakes she'd made in the past, so she shook off the memories.

"You called it, that was amazing," she said, pushing her plate away and sitting back with a sigh. "I'll need to double my workouts if I keep eating like this."

He scowled and shook his head. "You look perfectly fine the way you are."

Fine wasn't exactly flattering, but that didn't stop her from blushing. "Thanks again for dinner," she said, trying to change the subject. "I should probably head back home."

"All right," he agreed, gesturing for Maria to bring their bill. "If you have time, it might be nice to take a walk up to the top of the bluff first. A short walk will help your food digest, making room for dessert."

She caught her breath, thinking that a walk to the top of the bluff and dessert sounded like something more intimate than a friendly meal. Or was she overreacting?

She needed to get a grip. His brain was probably foggy from sheer exhaustion and he just wanted to keep active so he wouldn't fall asleep.

She took a deep breath to calm her racing heart. "Sure. That sounds fun," she said lightly.

Ryan smiled and quickly signed off on the bill. Before he could say anything more, though, his cell phone rang. He stared at the screen for a moment, before lifting his gaze to hers. "It's the hospital," he said with obvious regret. "I'm sorry, I'll need to take this call."

"Oh, no, it's not Emma, is it?" she asked, leaning forward in concern.

"I'll find out," he promised, pushing the button on his phone to connect to the caller. "This is Ryan Murphy," he said in a crisp, professional tone.

Cassie knew she shouldn't be listening to Ryan's side of the conversation—after all, there were rules about patient privacy. But she couldn't bear the thought of something happening to Emma. Or to any of their other tiny patients. Each baby in their care offered hope for the future.

"Discontinue her feedings immediately and get a chest X-ray, stat," Ryan said. "I'll be in to check on her and to write more orders shortly."

The way his eyes darkened with regret made her stomach clench. "What happened to Emma?" she demanded, fearing the worst.

"She aspirated some of her tube feeding while having a seizure," he admitted grimly. "I'm sorry, but I'll need to go in. I want to review her X-ray myself."

"I want to go with you," Cassie protested, rising to her feet. But then she let out a heavy breath. "But I can't. She doesn't belong to me yet."

"Give me your number," he urged, pulling out his phone. "I'll call you with an update."

"Really?" She readily gave him her number, watching with awe as he programmed her name into his phone. "Thank you, I really appreciate it."

Ryan slipped his phone back into his pocket. "Come on, I'll walk you back to your car."

"No, just go and take care of Emma," she said, putting her hand on his arm to stop him. For a moment his gaze dropped to her hand, before lifting up to look into her eyes, and she had to fight the urge to throw herself into his arms. "My car is only three blocks away. Emma needs you more than I do."

He hesitated, and then gave a brief nod. "All right. Take care, Cassandra." He leaned over to brush her mouth with his in a kiss so brief she thought she imagined it. "I'll call you later."

Speechless, she watched him stride off toward his car, lightly pressing her fingertips to her tingling lips.

He'd kissed her. She had no idea why, but he'd kissed her!

And she knew, without a doubt, that he'd call her, too, the minute he had an update about Emma's condition.

She was definitely in over her head, because there was no denying she couldn't wait to talk to Ryan or to see him again.

Ryan forced himself to concentrate on driving, instead of reliving their brief but electric kiss. What had possessed him to kiss her like that? It was as if his hard-won control had abandoned him. He'd wanted desperately to kiss her, so he had. In a public place no less.

What if someone had seen them?

But even the thought of Shana-like rumors rippling through the hospital wasn't enough to make him regret his action. How could it?

Every cell in his body wanted to kiss Cassie again,

a proper kiss, deep and intimate. The type of kiss that could lead to more.

But he couldn't turn his back on his patients either. Matthew was apparently stuck in a touchy delivery so Sheri had called him for help. He didn't mind, because waiting could prove deadly.

Well, he minded leaving Cassie, but his needs weren't important right now. If Emma ended up with aspiration pneumonia, she'd end up staying on the ventilator longer.

Not to mention that if the bacteria grew in her lungs and transferred into her bloodstream, the overwhelming infection could kill her.

He tightened his grip on the steering wheel. No way was he about to let that happen.

Ryan made it to the hospital in ten minutes and as he strode into the neonatal intensive care unit the staff gaped at the fact that he was wearing casual clothes, but he ignored them, heading straight over to Emma's warmer.

"I'm sorry to call you back in, Dr. Ryan," Sheri said, looking flustered. "I pulled up her chest X-ray on the computer monitor, the way you asked me to."

"I don't mind," he assured her. He washed his hands at the sink and then turned toward the nurse. "Can I borrow your stethoscope?"

"Sure." Sheri handed it over and he took the time to listen to Emma's lungs before giving the stethoscope back and taking a seat at the computer.

"There's a small amount of atelectasis in the base of her right lung," he said, battling a wave of helplessness. "Her breath sounds are diminished in that area, too. I'm going to order respiratory therapy treatments

for her as well as antibiotics. Roll her onto her left side
a bit, so that her lung can expand."

"All right," Sheri agreed. "Anything else?"

He stared blindly at the computer screen for a long
minute, wishing there was more he could do for Emma.
But at this point there wasn't. All he and Cassie could
do was to hope and pray the baby girl would continue
to fight.

He'd failed to save his wife and son, but he was determined not to fail Emma.

No matter what.

CHAPTER SIX

WHEN HER PHONE RANG, Cassie tossed her mystery book aside and shot off the sofa. A whole hour had passed since Ryan had left her to go to the hospital and she was anxious to know what was going on. "Hello, Ryan?"

"Yes, it's me. I'm leaving the hospital shortly, but wanted you to know that Emma's condition has been stabilized for now. The next twenty-four hours will be critical for her, though."

She momentarily closed her eyes, letting out a sigh of relief. "I'm so glad you were able to go in to take care of her. She deserves the best."

"I'm glad you're not upset that I had to leave," he countered. "Not all women are as understanding."

"That's just stupid," she said, suspecting he was speaking from experience. From the nurse he'd dated last year? Or from his wife? Didn't matter, she told herself firmly. "What did Emma's chest X-ray show?"

"A small collapsed area in her right lower lung," he said. "I'm hoping that with the antibiotics and respiratory therapy treatments, we'll be able to prevent full-blown pneumonia. The worst part is that her feedings have to be stopped for a while."

"Oh, no," she said with a sigh. Poor Emma wouldn't

gain much weight without being fed, but the risk was too high. "Thanks so much for calling me. Now go home and get some rest."

"I will, if you will," he said in that sexy, low, husky tone of his. "I'll give you a call in the morning."

"Okay. Goodnight, Ryan."

"Goodnight, Cassandra."

The way he said her full name in his husky voice made her want to stay on the phone with him forever. She disconnected from the call and then quickly added Ryan's name and number to her contact list. Why had he mentioned calling her in the morning? To give her an update on Emma's condition?

Or because he wanted to see her again?

She shook her head at her own foolishness. Ryan had made it clear he wasn't ready for a relationship. And she wasn't either. Her heart was still raw from the way Evan had trampled all over it. She really needed to stop microanalyzing Ryan's every move. Still, forgetting about him long enough to fall asleep wasn't easy.

And, of course, Ryan popped into her mind first thing in the morning. She needed to rein in her emotions. She and Ryan were friends, nothing more.

Besides, the last thing she needed was to be hurt by another man. Discovering Evan had cheated on her had been brutally painful. Not to mention the fact that she might not be able to have children of her own.

And Ryan clearly loved children. Hadn't he practically admitted that while they'd been in the elevator with Emma?

She has us. We care about her.

Cassie leaped out of bed, anxious to jump-start her day. She was worried about Emma, so she needed to keep busy. Since she'd promised herself she'd go for a run to work off the Swiss mushroom burger, she donned her running clothes and headed outside. Okay, so maybe she didn't exactly double her mileage but she ran a total of three miles and felt much better afterwards.

Saturday mornings were normally reserved for cleaning. She ate a quick breakfast of scrambled eggs and toast, and then decided there was no point in showering until she'd finished cleaning. She tossed a load of laundry into the machine and then began the tedious task of scrubbing her bathroom.

The sky outside had grown more cloudy, so she turned on the radio to listen for the weather report. Sure enough, there was a chance of thunderstorms rolling in, but not until later that afternoon. After finishing in her bathroom, she started on the tiny kitchen. She was singing along to a song on the radio when her phone rang. She tossed the sponge into the sink, dried her hands on the seat of her jeans and reached for the phone, her heart skipping when she saw Ryan's name on the screen.

"Hello?"

"Good morning, Cassie," Ryan greeted her. "Hope I'm not calling too early."

"Of course not," she said, glancing at the time. It was ten-thirty. She'd already gone for a run, cleaned her bathroom and finished two loads of laundry over the past two and a half hours. "I hope you were able to get a good night's sleep."

There was a brief pause and she wondered if that was too personal a question. Friends, remember? They were friends.

"I did, thanks," he finally said. "I don't have an update yet on Emma, but I'm sure I'll hear from Matthew soon."

"You read my mind," she teased. "I was going to ask how she was doing."

"I'll let you know as soon as I do," he promised. "Do you have any plans for your day off?"

No way was she going to confess that all she was doing was cleaning, which was nearly finished anyway. "Nothing special," she said slowly.

"I thought maybe we could head down to the park, see if we can find the woman we believe is connected to Emma. It's possible she might live close by."

Ridiculous to be disappointed that he had an ulterior motive for getting together. Friends, she reminded herself. They were friends. "Sure, why not? Although you have to know the chances of us just stumbling across her are slim to none."

"Maybe, but I bet we'll run into her sooner than later. How much time do you need?"

"Give me an hour," Cassie said, glancing at her kitchen. Surely finishing up in there wouldn't take long. "Where do you want to meet?"

"I'll pick you up," Ryan said.

It was on the tip of her tongue to argue, but she reminded herself that this wasn't a date. "Okay. I live in the apartments on Oakdale Drive. The third building. Apartment 302."

"All right, I'll see you in an hour."

Cassie set down her phone and rushed to finish cleaning her kitchen before jumping into the shower. She used the blow-dryer on her hair, even though she knew the humidity would eventually wreak havoc with it anyway.

Still, she wanted to look nice for Ryan, even if her long sleek hair would only last for an hour.

She pulled on a skirt, wincing a bit at her pale legs. One would think that with her dark hair she'd tan easily, but she didn't. A minute after she finished applying a light coat of makeup, the sound of her door buzzer echoed through the apartment.

Her heart stuttered and her stomach clenched with nerves, but she went over to the intercom to let him in.

He knocked at her door barely a minute later and she looped her purse over her shoulder before walking over to open the door. "Good morning," she greeted him. "I'm ready."

His blue eyes swept over her, glinting with approval. "You look amazing, Cassandra," he murmured.

She licked her suddenly dry lips. "Thanks," she murmured. "So do you." Oh, boy, what was wrong with her? She was acting like this was a date.

His gaze held hers for a long second, as if remembering their brief kiss. Or maybe that was just her memory working overtime. He stepped back, giving her room to leave her apartment. She released her pent-up breath and wondered if she was crazy to spend her day off with Ryan.

She already liked him too much already. And she couldn't bear the thought of giving him the power to hurt her. After all, his last relationship hadn't worked out, either.

No, she couldn't allow herself to become emotionally involved with Ryan. The nurses called him the Heartbreaker for a reason.

She wasn't sure she'd survive another emotional train wreck.

* * *

Ryan nearly swallowed his tongue when he saw Cassie standing there, looking breathtakingly beautiful.

He was playing with fire, but at the moment he couldn't seem to bring himself to care if he got burned.

"So, did Dr. Matthew call you back about Emma?"

He nodded. "Yes, she's doing pretty well. Her chest X-ray looks a little better, so I think the respiratory therapy treatments are working." He held the door open for her as they headed outside. "As I said before, the next twenty-four hours are critical. If she can turn the corner, she'll do great."

"I'm glad to hear that," Cassie said. Then her mouth gaped open when he crossed over to pull open the passenger-side door of his sporty cherry-red convertible. "You have a convertible?" she squeaked.

"Yes, I hope you don't mind," he said, glancing at her long hair. He remembered how Victoria hadn't liked the wind messing up her hair. "I can put the top up if you prefer."

"No way! I've always wanted to ride in a convertible." He watched in amusement as she rooted through her purse to find a hair tie. Pulling her hair back into a ponytail didn't take long. "This is going to be fun," she declared, sliding into the passenger seat.

Ryan smiled, closing the door behind her. Cassie was so different from Victoria, which made her dangerously attractive.

He hadn't been with a woman in a long time and forced himself to remember that Cassie wouldn't appreciate being used for sex. Truthfully, the idea didn't sit well with him, either. She deserved a man who would love and cherish her and little Emma.

Someone better than him. He didn't deserve a second chance. He hadn't loved Victoria the way he should have loved his wife, and his son had died because of it. Oh, he'd blamed Victoria, too, for becoming addicted to painkillers, but deep down he knew that he was the one at fault.

For not loving her enough.

For not noticing her addiction.

For not being home when she and his son had needed him.

He shook off the sobering thoughts with an effort. Ryan knew he'd need to find a way to keep his distance from Cassie. A task far easier said than done.

As he drove to the park, she lifted her face to the sky as if enjoying the wind against her skin. "This is fabulous!" she exclaimed. "You must love this car."

"It's just a car," he said mildly, enjoying the rapture on her face. "But I'm glad you're having fun."

He parked at the base of the walking path that would lead up the bluff, looking over Lake Michigan. "Come on, let's take a walk."

She climbed out of the car. "Okay, but I think we can safely assume that the woman we're trying to find wouldn't try to walk up this path with her cane."

He shrugged, refusing to admit that this part of the day was strictly for the two of them. "I know, but we can head into town to search for her after you see the view. It's amazing."

"Lead the way," she said with a smile.

Dark clouds swirled overhead and he hoped the rain would hold off, at least for a while. Cassie didn't say much as they climbed up the bluff, but he didn't find her silence awkward or strained.

She was an easy person to be with. Beautiful, compelling and nurturing, an intoxicating combination.

"Wow, you were right," she whispered once they reached the top. "This view is incredible."

He nodded, although his attention was focused more on Cassie than the view. He didn't deserve her, but he wanted Cassie so much he ached. "I knew you'd like it. I'm surprised other people aren't up here, although maybe the rainclouds scared them away."

"Could be," she said, glancing up. "The weather report said the rain wouldn't come until two this afternoon, but those clouds look ominous."

"We'd better head back down," he murmured, hating to cut their time short. "Before the clouds let loose."

He caught her hand in his as they started their descent. Going down was faster than going up, and soon they were back in the convertible. "I'll put the top up," he said, reaching for the controls.

"Please, don't, it's not raining yet," she said, putting her hand on his arm.

Every nerve in his body went on alert at her touch. And at that moment he couldn't deny her anything. "All right, let's hope we don't get drenched. The car has to be in park before the mechanism will work to put the top up."

"We'll be fine," she assured him.

He fought with his chaotic emotions during the short ride back into town. A couple of sprinkles showered them as he parked. He closed up the car and slid out from behind the wheel. "Let's head over to Main Street."

"We'd better hurry." Cassie cast a glance up at

the clouds just as a rumble of thunder echoed above them. "Run!"

This time Cassie grabbed his hand as they ran down the road toward Main Street. They reached the safety of the canopy over the window of the ice-cream parlor just as a heavy sheet of rain poured from the sky.

Cassie laughed, not at all upset about the raindrops dampening her hair and skin. "We made it," she said breathlessly.

She was so beautiful, so warm and full of life that he couldn't help himself. He tugged her close, wrapped his arms around her and kissed her. A proper kiss. Delving deep into the sweet recesses of her mouth.

Kissing Cassie felt like nothing he'd experienced before. Like coming home.

And this time he didn't want to ever let her go.

Cassie gasped when Ryan pulled her in for a scorching kiss. She knew she should push him away, but her muscles melted against him, reveling in the desire that flared instantly between them.

This time he didn't settle for a chaste kiss, but angled his head and teased her lips until she opened for him, allowing him to deepen the intimacy.

His heady taste went straight to her brain, far more potent than whiskey or wine. He kissed her with a single-minded intensity that she'd never experienced before. Everything around them vanished. She was only aware of the smoldering heat of his mouth and the firmness and strength of his muscles beneath her exploring fingertips.

She wanted to stay in his arms, forever.

"Is that Dr. Ryan Murphy?" a woman nearby asked in a shocked voice. "Who is he kissing?"

It took a moment for the comment to register through the fiery heat, but once she realized people were talking about them, she pulled back, gulping in deep breaths of air. "We shouldn't be doing this," she whispered, resting her forehead on his broad chest. "People are watching."

The thundering beat of his heart gave her confidence that the impact of their kiss wasn't one-sided. "I'm sorry," he murmured, smoothing his hand down her back, which only made her regret the fact that they were wearing clothes. "Not for kissing you, but for dragging you into the Cedar Bluff gossip mill."

Despite feeling embarrassed, she couldn't help but let out a chuckle. She lifted her head and stepped back, despite the way she longed for him to sweep her back into his arms. "Maybe I'm the one who dragged you into the gossip mill," she said wryly. "After all, I'm the new kid in town."

He cupped her cheek with his hand and she leaned into his caress. "You have no idea how much I wish I had more to offer you, Cassandra," he said, regret shimmering from his eyes. "But I don't."

Her heart twisted at the seriousness of his tone and she knew he was reminding her about how his last relationship hadn't worked out. Was he still grieving his dead wife? Probably.

"I know," she said simply. She forced herself to take another step back, immediately missing his warmth. "It's probably better this way," she added. "Especially since we work together."

Ryan looked as if he wanted to say something more,

but she didn't want to hear any platitudes. Or, worse, find herself begging for anything he was willing to give.

Just remembering the devastation she'd gone through after suffering her second miscarriage and then listening as Evan had told his lover how glad he was that she'd lost the baby was enough to bring her to her senses. She hadn't been good enough for Evan, who was to say Ryan wouldn't get tired of her, too? Besides, Ryan didn't know about her inability to have children. Would he look at her differently once he knew the truth? The very thought was enough to convince her to put Ryan back into the friend category before things spiraled out of control.

Who was she kidding? They'd already spun out of control.

"How about we get some ice cream while we wait out the storm?" she suggested, hoping her desperation wasn't too obvious.

"Sure," he agreed.

They ducked out from beneath the awning over the window to head inside the ice-cream parlor. There were a few other customers inside and she could feel their curious gazes boring into her as they reviewed the ice-cream selections.

"I'll have double-chocolate fudge," she said, striving to sound normal. After that toe-curling kiss, and Ryan's emotional withdrawal, she was tempted to wallow in an entire vat of chocolate.

"Make that two," he told the woman behind the counter.

Once they had their dishes of ice cream, Cassie wanted nothing more than to leave. "I think the rain is lightening up," she said, gesturing toward the window. "Why don't we run over to the coffee shop next door?"

"Sounds good," Ryan agreed. She tried to ignore his closeness as they darted over to the coffee shop.

She noticed the cane woman seated in the booth farthest in the back right away. Grabbing the distraction with both hands, she headed straight toward her with steely determination.

"Hi, my name is Cassie Jordan. Do you remember meeting me outside the neonatal ICU?"

She looked shocked but recovered quickly. "Yes, of course."

"Do you mind telling me your name?" Cassie pressed, sensing Ryan coming up to stand supportively beside her. "Do you know Emma's mother?"

"My name is Lydia and, no, I don't know anyone named Emma." The woman couldn't hold Cassie's gaze and she suspected the woman was lying. But why?

"Lydia, please know that I care about Emma, very much. And having some sort of medical history on Emma's mother would help us take better care of the baby. Do you understand? Emma's mother isn't in any trouble, we just want to ask her a few questions, that's all."

For a moment Cassie thought she'd gotten through to the woman, whose indecision was clearly reflected in her eyes, but Lydia abruptly shook her head and leaned hard on the table, pushing herself to her feet. She grabbed her cane. "I'm sorry, but I don't know anything. I can't help you."

Cassie glanced up at Ryan, feeling helpless. They were so close, but the woman wasn't talking.

"Ms. Lydia, please know that we are taking very good care of Emma. She's had a few setbacks, but I assure you I plan to do everything possible to help Emma get better."

Cassie thought she saw a flash of gratitude in Lydia's eyes before she moved past them to head for the door, obviously intending to leave, despite the rain.

And Cassie couldn't think of a way to stop her.

CHAPTER SEVEN

RYAN SCOWLED WITH frustration as Lydia left the coffee shop. He knew she was connected to Emma in some way, most likely by blood. He was convinced she was either Emma's grandmother or her great-aunt, despite her denials to the contrary.

But there wasn't much he could do, considering they were pushing Lydia for information she legally didn't have to give.

"She knows something," Cassie murmured, dropping down into a chair and staring morosely at her melting ice cream. "But for some reason she doesn't trust us."

He nodded, remaining on his feet because he didn't trust himself, not around Cassie. The memory of holding her in his arms and kissing her was still too fresh in his mind. The double-chocolate fudge ice cream was a poor substitute for her sweet taste.

"And she didn't give us her last name either," Cassie continued. "Which makes me think that she's related to Emma's mother closely enough that we might be able to figure out the connection if she'd told us."

"Good point," he agreed. Reluctantly, he took the seat across from Cassie, trying not to show his reaction to her nearness. His heart rate still hadn't returned to normal after their kiss and her warm vanilla scent was embedded in his mind.

He tried to think of something to say that would make her feel better, but his brain cells were foggy with desire.

Cassie only ate about half of her ice cream before pushing her container aside. "Well, I guess our plan didn't work out after all, although it was worth a try." Her tone was offhand, but she didn't meet his gaze as she stood. "I think I'll head home. Thanks for the ice cream."

He shot to his feet, desperate to keep her with him. "Wait, you can't walk in the rain, I'll drive you home."

"Actually, I'd rather walk," she said, finally meeting his gaze, her eyes filled with steely determination. "It's warm outside, I won't melt. And I'd like to be alone. Take care, Ryan, see you around."

Panic hit hard and he reached out a hand to stop her but she shook him off and hurried to the door. Helplessly, he watched her leave, wishing for the millionth time that things could be different.

Sinking down in his seat, he sighed and dropped his head into his hands. His body craved her warmth, but his brain knew that letting Cassie go was the right thing to do. She deserved the best.

Someone far better than him. He'd never told a single soul about how he'd planned to file for divorce from Victoria. But then she'd announced she was pregnant and he'd shoved aside the idea of divorcing her. For one thing, he loved kids and had been thrilled at the thought of having a child. Plus, he'd come from a broken home and couldn't bear the idea of his child growing up under the same circumstances. So he'd decided there had to be a way to make things work out between them.

Five months later, he'd come home late one night to find Victoria sitting behind the wheel of the car, her skin cold and gray. The moment he'd touched the roundness of her abdomen he'd known she'd been dead for several hours.

Taking their son with her.

It wasn't until he'd found the empty prescription bottle in the cup holder next to her that he'd realized she'd still been taking oxycodone. Her surgery had been several months before she'd become pregnant, so finding them had been a terrible shock.

The police had right away assumed the worst, thinking that he'd either forced her to take the pills or had abused her to the point she'd needed to take them. The thought of suicide hit hard, but then he discovered the doctor's name on the pill bottle wasn't the same as her orthopedic surgeon's. The police had agreed to look into it. But the doctor's name was Oliver Stevenson and the address had turned out to be a vacant building.

Leaving no leads for Detective Trammel to follow.

He sighed and pulled himself together, taking the time to throw away their unfinished dishes of ice cream before heading outside. The rain had slowed to a steady drizzle, so logically he knew Cassie would be fine.

But he followed the path to her apartment building anyway, frowning when he didn't see her walking along the sidewalk.

Where had she gone? He reached for his phone and called her, but she didn't answer. He scowled and listened to her voice-mail greeting.

"Hi, you've reached Cassie. Leave a message and I'll call you back. Thanks!"

"Cassie, this is Ryan. Please call me back and let me know you've made it home safely. Thank you."

He scowled and shoved the phone back into his pocket, before making a U-turn and heading home.

When he pulled in the driveway, he stared at the large house Victoria had insisted they build, struck by the sudden urge to put the house up for sale. Yeah, the housing market sucked, but you couldn't sell what you didn't list. Besides, so what if he took a loss?

The place had never felt like home anyway.

With renewed determination he called a real estate agent and left a message about wanting to put his house up for sale. Then he called the hospital to check on Emma. She remained stable, thankfully showing no sign of running a fever.

Then he sat back and stared at his phone, willing Cassie to return his call.

But as the hours ticked by she didn't.

Cassie spent the rest of her Saturday with her friend Gloria, trying to forget about Ryan, at least for a little while. Gloria was happy to oblige. They ordered Chinese food and enjoyed a chick-flick marathon.

Her heart raced when she realized Ryan had called, but she couldn't bring herself to return his call. For one thing, why on earth would he think she hadn't made it home? This was Cedar Bluff, not the north side of Milwaukee. Sure, they had some crime, but nothing that would prevent her from getting home all right. He was simply being ridiculous and she feared that if she called him back she'd throw herself at him, begging for another kiss.

Not a good idea.

"This was great, Gloria. Thanks for picking me up and inviting me over," Cassie said, when the last movie finished. "I should head home, I have to work tomorrow."

"Poor thing," Gloria said with mock pity. "I'm off tomorrow for my brother's graduation party. You could come before work if you want, it starts at noon."

Cassie wrinkled her nose. "You'll be busy with your family. I'll just sleep in and then go to work."

"The invitation stands if you change your mind," Gloria assured her.

"Okay, I'll think about it," Cassie agreed. The last thing she needed was to wallow around her apartment all morning, thinking about Ryan. Maybe going to the graduation party would be a good way to keep from ruminating over things she couldn't change.

"Do you want me to drive you home?" Gloria asked, as she headed toward the door.

Cassie rolled her eyes. "Don't be silly, we live in the same apartment complex. I'm just two buildings down."

"Okay, maybe I'll see you tomorrow." Gloria gave her a quick hug and then closed and locked the door behind her.

Cassie had to force herself not to call Ryan as she trudged home. The urge to connect with him was strong so she mentally made a list of things to do once she was approved to be a foster parent.

The first thing on her list was to look for a two-bedroom apartment. She wasn't sure how many two-bedroom apartments were available at the moment and made a mental note to check with the manager as soon as possible. Plus, she had to convince the landlord to transfer her lease as it wasn't up until November. Once she had a second bedroom she could decorate for a new baby.

For Emma? God, she hoped so.

She knew she needed to be realistic. As much as she longed to have Emma, she had to be prepared for the fact that she might not get approved in time. At least she'd be ready for the next baby that needed her.

A baby that she wouldn't be able to have on her own.

That night, she shut her phone off so that she wouldn't be tempted to call Ryan. Or answer his call if he tried again.

She tossed and turned most of the night, leaving her feeling cranky and out of sorts when she switched her phone back on the next morning. She debated going over to Gloria's parents' place on the lake, but decided she wasn't really in the mood for company.

When her phone rang, she jumped, expecting the caller to be Ryan. But instead it was the hospital number. Even if it was Ryan calling from the hospital, he might have news about Emma, so she quickly picked it up. "Hello?"

"Cassie? This is Diane. One of our day-shift nurses started throwing up and needed to go home. Would you be willing to start your shift early? We could really use the help."

"Of course," Cassie agreed. "I can be there in fifteen minutes."

"Thanks so much," Diane said in a rush. "The nurse who left to go home sick was taking care of Emma and the newest baby from the other day, Daniel. So at least you'll be familiar with one of the patients."

Knowing that she would get to take care of Emma made all the difference in the world. Her mood brightened considerably. "Great. I'll be there soon." Cassie quickly disconnected from the call and hurried to change into her scrubs.

It wasn't until she was walking into the hospital, that she wondered if Ryan was working today, too.

Her cheerfulness dimmed a little as she realized how difficult it would be to work alongside him as if they hadn't shared that sizzling kiss. This was the reason it was better not to date your colleagues. When things fell apart, everything was affected, both your work life and home life.

All the more reason not to venture down the path of temptation again.

Cassie quickly swiped her badge to get into the unit and then went to punch in at the time clock. She hurried over to Emma's warmer, grateful to see that Daniel's warmer was immediately adjacent to Emma's. Both babies were on ventilators, but as she quickly reviewed the notes it was clear Daniel had been weaned down to the point he was ready to have the tube out.

"Thanks again for coming in," Diane said, hurrying over. "Do you have any questions? I've been keeping an eye on these two until you could get here."

"Looks like Daniel's ready to get rid of his ventilator. Who's the intensivist on call today?"

"Dr. Ryan was here earlier. He's in a delivery right now, but he should be back soon." Diane didn't seem to notice how Cassie had gone still at hearing Ryan's name. "Do you want me to double-check the drips with you?"

"Ah, sure, that would be great." Cassie forced her brain to go into work mode, even though she was secretly thrilled Ryan was working today.

Once she'd caught up with what had transpired over the past twenty-four to thirty-six hours, she hovered over Emma. "Hey, sweetpea, how are you? I'm going to be here with you for twelve hours today, isn't that great? And then tomorrow I'm going to enroll in foster-care classes. I'm fighting for you, sweetpea. All you need to do is to get better, okay?"

Of course Emma didn't respond, but Cassie didn't care. She stroked Emma's cheek, hoping to soothe the baby. She felt a bit disheartened to realize they'd had to raise the vent settings since Friday, but, of course, they couldn't risk the chance she might develop pneumonia.

She managed to keep busy for the next hour or so, between double-checking other nurse's medications and caring for her two babies. Every free moment she had she spent with Emma.

"Good afternoon, Cassandra, you're here early."

Ryan's deep voice made her shiver in awareness, despite the stern talking-to she'd given herself before her shift.

"Amy got sick, so they called me in to cover," she said, striving to keep her tone steady. "How does Emma's chest X-ray look? I thought her lungs sounded pretty good, but maybe I missed something."

"Her X-ray looks much better," Ryan said, glancing down at Emma with a smile. "Her lower lobe has expanded back to normal, and her breath sounds are definitely clearing up."

"Wonderful news," she said in relief. "I've been so worried about her."

"I know." Ryan stepped closer and dropped his voice. "I was worried about you, too. Why didn't you return my call?"

He was so close she found it hard to breathe normally. She took a hasty step back, knowing she didn't owe him any explanations, but feeling compelled to tell him anyway. "I spent time with my friend, Gloria. You remember her, she's the one who took care of Emma in the ER until we got down there."

"So she came and picked you up?" he asked.

"I actually ran into her and she offered to drive me home. We live in the same apartment complex but in different buildings." The alarm on Daniel's vent went off, indicating a high peak pressure, one of the signs that he was trying to overbreathe the vent. "Have you had a chance to examine Daniel? I think he's ready to be extubated."

"Let me double-check his weaning parameters." Ryan crossed over to Daniel's warmer. She followed, determined to keep things on a professional level between them.

No more mooning over him. And definitely no more kissing.

"You're right, these look good. Call the respiratory therapist to help me extubate him."

Grateful for something productive to do, Cassie did as Ryan asked. Jason was the respiratory therapist on duty today, and he promised to be right over.

Cassie concentrated on documenting in Daniel's chart, silently admitting it was an easy way to avoid Ryan.

"Hi, Cassie," Jason said as he approached. "I hear Daniel is about to get rid of that nasty tube."

"Absolutely," she agreed. "Dr. Ryan wants to extubate whenever you're ready."

The procedure of removing a breathing tube didn't take long and Daniel let out a loud cry as soon as the tube was gone. Ryan picked Daniel up and propped the baby against his shoulder. Ryan rubbed the boy's back as if he had a dozen children of his own.

"There, now, you're going to be much happier now that you can yell at us, aren't you?" he said with a wry smile. "Trust me, that crying is good for your lungs so don't hold back. Just let it all out. We can take it."

Cassie stared at him in shock, her heart melting like butter on a griddle as she watched Ryan caring for Daniel. Did he want children of his own? Or not? He should, because he'd make a great father.

Daniel quieted down, resting against Ryan's chest.

"You're a natural father," she murmured. "You must want children of your own."

The light in Ryan's eyes dimmed a bit, although he nodded. "Someday," he agreed.

Someday? What did that mean? Someday, as in once he was ready to risk having a relationship? Or someday, as in a long time from now?

Was he still grieving over his dead wife?

Her stomach clenched with worry. Ryan wanted children, babies she probably wasn't able to have. But did that desire extend to Emma? She had no idea.

Weary of her mental tug-of-war, she turned away. Staying away from Ryan was better for her in the long run.

When Emma's monitor alarm went off, she hurried over, relaxing a bit when she noticed that the baby had somehow dislodged one of the heart leads.

"False alarm," she said, when she saw Ryan had returned Daniel to his warmer and was crossing over to Emma. "One of her leads came loose."

He nodded, but didn't look in a hurry to leave. She took a breath, wishing he would just go away and leave her alone. She didn't want to feel all torn up inside like this. When the phone next to Emma's computer rang, she pounced on it. "This is Cassie in the NNICU, may I help you?"

"Cass? It's Gloria." Her friend's voice was thick with tears. "My brother, Trey, is here in the ER. I think he overdosed on pain meds. The police are investigating."

"What? He overdosed on pain meds and the police are there?" Cassie said, her gaze clashing with Ryan's. "I don't understand. Where did he get pain meds?"

"I don't know, but his condition is pretty serious. I know you're working but if you have time to come down to the ER, I'd appreciate it."

"I'll come as soon as I can," Cassie promised.

"Who overdosed on pain meds?" Ryan demanded.

"Gloria Reynolds's brother, Trey," she admitted. Before she could say anything more Ryan spun on his heel and strode out of the unit, no doubt heading down to the ER.

She frowned at his retreating figure. Why was Ryan heading down to the ER? She couldn't come up with a single reason.

She turned back toward Emma, knowing that she couldn't leave her tiny patients, no matter how much she wanted to follow Ryan.

CHAPTER EIGHT

RYAN JOGGED DOWN the stairs to the ER, determined to talk to the police investigating Trey Reynolds's overdose. He desperately wanted to know where Gloria's brother had gotten his pain meds.

He knew the police wouldn't want to tell him anything, but he hoped that if Detective Trammel was there, he'd get something out of the detective. Ryan had a sick feeling in his gut that there was a connection between this young man's overdose and Victoria's death.

Surely Detective Trammel knew it, too?

No one questioned why he was there when he walked through the arena of the ER over to the trauma bay. He stopped short when he saw the ER team working with controlled chaos to save the young man's life. He was impressed at how quickly yet efficiently they performed live-saving measures. They'd already inserted a breathing tube and were in the process of giving medication into his stomach to prevent whatever pills he'd taken from being absorbed into his bloodstream.

In the corner of the room, Gloria, the ER nurse who'd been at the triage desk when Emma had been dropped off, stood with her hands over her mouth and tears trailing down her cheeks. He knew all about the helpless guilt of not being able to prevent the tragedy.

But before he could walk over there he caught a glimpse of Detective Trammel on the other side of the room.

Without hesitation, he headed over to where the detective and a uniformed officer were standing, giving the trauma team a wide berth to stay out of their way.

"Detective Trammel," he said with a nod. "I understand you have another pain med overdose?"

The detective scowled. "How did you hear about this case?"

"Through a friend," he acknowledged, refusing to feel guilty for eavesdropping on Cassie's conversation with Gloria. "Do you know what physician's name is listed on the prescription bottle?"

Trammel's expression darkened further. "Look, Dr. Murphy, I can't discuss the details of my investigation with you."

"Can't or won't?" Ryan challenged, refusing to give up. "I'm not asking for a full report on your investigation, I just want to validate the physician's name on the prescription bottle. Was it Oliver Stevenson?"

The uniformed cop standing beside Detective Trammel jerked his head around in surprise, giving away the truth. Ryan couldn't help feeling a surge of satisfaction when Trammel looked irritated for a moment, but then gave a brief nod.

"I knew it," Ryan muttered. Oliver Stevenson was the same physician who'd ordered the pain meds for Victoria. But her surgeon had been a different guy by the name of Dr. Geoff Avery. At the time, that knowledge had haunted him and he'd looked high and low for Stevenson.

Without finding a single trace of him.

"Before you get too excited at the connection, remember that we weren't able to find this alleged doctor anywhere," Trammel said dryly. "If you recall, the address of his so-called doctor's office turned out to be nothing more than a vacant building at the end of a strip mall outside Madison. And there was no one listed in the state of Wisconsin by that name."

Ryan scowled. "Yeah, I remember. But at least you know this young man's prescription is fraudulent, too. There has to be some sort of group coordinating getting these scripts into the hands of people who are willing to pay for them."

"Maybe, but that doesn't mean we're going to have an easy time tracking down the source of the fraud," Trammel argued. "This could be a legit pain doctor who happened to move to a different office building or it could be someone who has stolen this physician's DEA number."

His brief satisfaction evaporated quickly, because Trammel was right. Ryan found himself leaning toward a stolen DEA number, but how on earth would they prove it? "I could help," he began to offer, but Trammel lifted up his hand to stop him.

"I understand your personal interest in this case, Dr. Murphy, but since I don't tell you how to take care of sick babies, I'd appreciate it if you wouldn't tell me how to run my investigation."

There wasn't a rational argument against his request, so Ryan forced himself to nod before turning away.

"Dr. Murphy?" Trammel called.

He turned to face the detective. "Yes?"

"I will let you know the outcome of our investigation," Trammel assured him, "once we have proof."

"Thanks," he murmured. Ryan knew he'd never be able to find closure related to Victoria's and his unborn son's deaths until he could help bring the perpetrators to justice.

But right now the best way to do that was to allow the detective to do his job. After all, he himself wasn't a cop. Ryan understood that Trammel had resources he didn't.

Ryan carefully made his way back around to the other side of the room to where Gloria was watching the resuscitative efforts being performed on her brother. The fact that she was here at all was unusual, but obviously being a nurse in the ER worked in her favor.

"Is there someone I can call for you?" he asked, his tone full of sympathy.

She slowly shook her head. "No, my parents are outside in the waiting room, but I can't talk to them yet. Not until I know more. Not until I know if Trey's going to be all right."

"What happened?"

Gloria sniffed and swiped at her tears. "He plays sports, football and baseball. I knew he hurt his shoulder late in the football season and was seeing one of the orthopedic surgeons, but he never had surgery, so I thought he was fine. But then one of his friends mentioned how he reinjured that same shoulder playing baseball last weekend. I think he must have been taking pain meds all along without any of us knowing."

Ryan's gut twisted. Trey's story was all too familiar. "Which surgeon?"

"Dr. Francowitz," she said.

Not the same orthopedic surgeon Victoria had used, which wasn't surprising, since orthopedic surgeons who worked on shoulders didn't normally also do Achilles tendons. He glanced back at the young man in the trauma bay, silently willing him to make it.

He couldn't bear the thought of losing another young life to an overdose of narcotic pain medication.

Cassie found a nurse to cover her two patients so she could dash briefly down to the ER to see Trey. When she arrived in the trauma bay it appeared the staff were finishing their resuscitation efforts. The rhythmic beat of Trey's heart on the monitor over his bed was reassuring. She swept her gaze over the room, finding Gloria standing well out of the way, with Ryan at her side.

"Gloria," she said, rushing over to give her friend a hug. "How is he doing?"

"They're getting ready to transfer him up to the ICU," Gloria said, returning her hug.

Cassie glanced up at Ryan with a questioning gaze. She wasn't sure why Ryan had come down here—did he have a previous relationship with Gloria? Was Gloria the nurse he'd been seeing when things hadn't worked out? She tried to squelch the flash of jealousy. "Then his condition has been stabilized, right?"

"Yes, from what I can tell," Ryan agreed.

"They intubated him and gave him charcoal to help get rid of the pills that might be still in his stomach," Gloria said in a low tone. "The biggest question is whether or not he'll wake up. It could be that he's suffered brain damage."

"He's young, Gloria." Cassie put a reassuring arm around her friend's shoulder. "I'm sure he'll be fine."

"I hope so," Gloria said in a strained voice. "He has his whole life ahead of him. He's supposed to attend college in the fall…" Her voice trailed off and her eyes filled with tears.

"I know," Cassie said, glancing up at Ryan helplessly. Ryan didn't offer Gloria physical comfort, which gave Cassie a small measure of relief. Still, Ryan's reaction to the situation was odd.

They stood for a few minutes until the trauma team wheeled Trey out of the room.

"I guess I better go talk to my parents." Gloria's tone was grim.

Cassie nodded. "I'm sorry, Gloria, but I have to run back upstairs to my patients. I'll check on you again during my lunch hour. In the meantime, keep me updated on how he's doing, okay?"

Gloria sniffed and dabbed her eyes again. "Okay, thanks, Cass. You're a great friend."

Cassie gave her another quick hug before turning away.

"I'll head back upstairs with you," Ryan said, falling into step beside her.

Cassie waited until they were far enough away that Gloria couldn't overhear their conversation. "Do you really think her brother will be all right?"

Ryan hesitated and shrugged. "I honestly don't know. He has youth on his side, and he was given very good medical care. But the result will depend on how long his brain went without oxygen."

Cassie knew he was right. "Such a waste," she said

under her breath. "I just don't understand how this kind of thing can happen."

Ryan's gaze was grim. "Me, either."

As they waited for the elevator, she glanced up at him curiously. "Ryan, why did you rush down here, like that?" she asked. "Did you go out with Gloria in the past? Do you know her younger brother?"

He shrugged but didn't meet her gaze. "No, I never dated Gloria and I don't know her brother, Trey. But I do have a special interest in narcotic-overdose cases," he finally said.

He did? Why? Cassie was ridiculously relieved to know he hadn't asked Gloria out, but she found she was more curious than ever. She wanted to ask more about why he cared so much about narcotic-overdose patients but two other staff members joined them, and when the elevator arrived the car was half-filled with people. They all rode together up to the third floor. She led the way into the NNICU, using her badge to get through the door, and then hurried over to Emma's warmer.

"How are Emma and Daniel doing?" she asked Christy, the nurse she'd asked to watch over them. "Any problems?"

"None at all," Christy assured her.

"Good, thanks for covering." Cassie glanced back at Ryan, wondering again why he had such a keen interest in narcotic-overdose patients. And even more strange, why he didn't seem willing to talk about it? Unless seeing Trey's young face had only reminded him of losing his wife?

It wasn't easy to focus on the issues at hand. Ryan's personal life wasn't any of her business. Hadn't she vowed to keep her distance? After all, he'd been the one who'd pulled away after their kiss.

So why was she still so drawn to him? The magnetic pull shimmering between them was so strong she doubted she'd be able to break the invisible bond.

And if she wasn't careful, he'd break her heart. Worse than Evan had.

"How is Daniel doing postextubation?" Ryan asked from behind her.

Once again, her pulse leapt at the husky sound of his voice. "He's doing great," she assured him. She moved away from him toward Daniel's warmer. "It's been about an hour since we pulled the tube. Do you want me to get a set of blood gases?"

"Yes, please." Ryan sat down at the computer and quickly entered the order.

Cassie busied herself with getting the supplies she'd need for the arterial blood gases. She didn't like having to poke the babies for lab work, but she knew the tests were needed to make the right medical decisions.

Thankfully she was able to get the arterial blood on the first try, although listening to Daniel's crying when she poked him wasn't easy. As soon as she'd finished holding pressure on the puncture site, she sent the blood off to the lab and then went over to lift him into her arms.

"There, there, big guy, you're fine. No more ouchies," she promised.

She could feel Ryan's penetrating gaze watching her with Daniel and it took every ounce of willpower she possessed not to turn around to face him, fearing her turbulent emotions would be reflected on her face.

Thankfully the arrival of Daniel's parents broke the

tense moment. As Cassie handed over their baby, Ryan gave them a quick update on Daniel's medical status.

Cassie slipped over to Emma's warmer, focusing her attention on the baby girl.

Emma was all alone in the world, just like *she* was. Oh, she had friends, but no family. Her parents had died when she was young and her grandparents had raised her. They'd passed away when she'd been in college. Being alone and vulnerable, she had been easy prey for Evan's fake charm.

Staring down at Emma, she knew she didn't miss Evan at all. But she missed the babies she hadn't been able to carry to term.

Emma F. Safe Haven was like a miracle dropped into her lap. A chance to have the family she'd always wanted. A chance to start over.

Maybe they weren't bonded by blood. But that didn't matter. The little girl was already the daughter of her heart.

Ryan tried to keep busy, but no matter what he was doing he found himself searching for Cassie. For a brief moment he'd considered telling her the truth about how he'd lost Victoria and his unborn son, but placing his burden on Cassie didn't seem fair. Especially as she was working.

Or maybe he was subconsciously avoiding the horror he might find in Cassie's eyes once she knew the truth.

He spent his downtime searching for Oliver Stevenson on the Wisconsin Department of Regulation and Licensing website, but of course there was no physician listed by that name. Just like there hadn't been three years ago.

Was this guy practicing without a license? Or was he practicing in another state? The DEA number had to be real or the pharmacy wouldn't have filled the script.

But what about out of state? Victoria's prescription had had a Madison address, so he hadn't broadened his search. But now he decided to check the bordering states of Minnesota, Michigan and Illinois. He found a couple of providers by that name, but none of them were pain specialists. Still, he wrote down their names and DEA numbers, determined to ask Trammel to verify if the number on both Trey's and Victoria's prescriptions was a match.

Cassie came over to stand beside him, and he quickly minimized the website. He noticed she glanced briefly at the names he'd written down, and shifted so that he partially blocked her view.

"How's Emma?" he asked, hoping to distract her.

She smiled. "Great. I was wondering if we couldn't start weaning her from the ventilator a bit?"

"I'm not sure that's a good idea," he said, true regret in his tone. "I want to see her come off that vent as much as you do, but I normally don't do much weaning after seven o'clock in the evening."

"I understand," Cassie murmured, her gaze full of obvious disappointment.

"If she's doing this well by tomorrow morning, I'll write the weaning orders," he promised. "That gives her another twenty-four hours of antibiotics."

She forced a smile and nodded. "Okay, that sounds like a good plan. The last thing I want is for her condition to take a turn for the worse."

When she turned away he reached out to grasp her arm, preventing her from leaving. "Have you figured out what your next steps are to becoming a foster parent?"

She glanced down at his hand, and then brought her gaze back up to meet his. "There are twelve classes I need to take once they approve my application."

"Twelve classes? That seems like a lot."

"I know. Too bad all parents don't have to take parenting classes, huh?" she said with a wry smile.

He nodded, thinking about the cases of child abuse they'd seen, thankfully not often.

"I can't sign up for the first class until tomorrow. The website won't accept sign-ups on the weekend," she added. "And I'm hoping that they'll approve my application fast."

"Can you sign up for all twelve classes right away?"

"I'm not sure, but even if I can, it might be too difficult anyway, since I have to work around my schedule or find a way to get off. Although that's not easy during the summer months when everyone else is off."

"Is there anything I can do to help?" he asked.

She shook her head and took a step back, severing the physical connection between them. He instantly missed her warmth. Her smile. Her laughter. "No. This is something I need to do myself."

He watched her walk back over to Emma's warmer, his heart aching with regret. He knew there was a tiny spot in his heart that had remained frozen ever since Victoria's and his son's deaths. He wasn't capable of loving Cassie the way she deserved.

So why did he long for her so desperately?

CHAPTER NINE

THE NEXT MORNING, Cassie woke up feeling energized, full of a new sense of purpose. Normally, she didn't look forward to Mondays—who did? But since it was a weekday, she was able to take the next steps in the process of becoming a foster parent. And even though there was a part of her that knew she was using the process as a way to forget about Ryan, she eagerly booted up her computer.

The sooner she signed up for the classes, the better her chances were of actually getting in.

When she'd read up on being a foster parent, she'd learned that safe-haven babies were able to go through the path from fostering to adopting much quicker than in other cases.

Of course there was always a six-month wait, in case the mother changed her mind.

Cassie couldn't deny that the thought of Emma's mother showing up and requesting custody was depressing. Especially since the baby had gone through narcotic withdrawal.

Still, anything was possible. For now, she needed to focus on the issues at hand, rather than worrying about the what-if scenarios.

As she ate breakfast, Cassie went to the Health and Human Services website to find the classes she needed. She double-clicked on the first one and prayed that it wasn't already full.

It wasn't and she quickly entered the required fields on the website, letting out a squeal as she hit enter. The hourglass spun in the center of the screen for what seemed like forever, before a message finally popped up on the screen.

"Accepted! I'm accepted in the first class!" Cassie jumped up and danced around her postage-stamp-sized kitchen.

Music blared from her phone, and Cassie danced over, her enthusiasm dimming as she noted the caller was Gloria.

She did her best to hide her elation over being accepted in the first class as she answered. "Hi, Gloria, how are you doing?" By the time she'd left work last night, Trey still hadn't woken up, although the ICU team had put him on a hypothermia protocol to preserve his brain function, much like they did for cardiac-arrest patients.

Trey really was getting the best medical care possible.

"Better this morning. They're going to start bringing Trey's temperature back up," Gloria said. "Once his temperature is within normal range, they'll back off on the sedation and we'll know if he'll wake up or not."

"I know it's hard, but you have to be strong for him and your family, Gloria," Cassie said encouragingly.

"I know. I'm trying," Gloria admitted.

"What do the neurologists think?" she asked.

"They won't say much one way or the other, but

based on how young he is, they're cautiously optimistic."

Of course the doctors wouldn't make promises they couldn't keep, but at the same time they didn't want families to lose hope either. "Do you want me to come and sit with you in the ICU?" she offered.

"No, my parents are here, so there's no need for you to come. I just wanted to give you an update. It's good news they're bringing him out of the hypothermia protocol."

"I agree," she assured her friend. "Keep in touch, Gloria."

"I will."

Cassie disconnected from the call, set her phone aside, and then returned to sit at her kitchen table in front of the computer. Before she could log back in to the site, her phone sang again.

This time Ryan's name popped up on the screen and despite the way her pulse jumped, she hesitated for a moment, gathering her defenses, before answering. "Hello?"

"Good morning, Cassandra. How are you?"

She strove to keep her voice steady. "I'm fine, Ryan, how are you? I hope your night on call wasn't too bad."

"I managed to get a little over four hours of sleep, so I can't complain."

"That's good." Their conversation was awkward, stilted, and she wished he'd get to the point already. She couldn't believe he'd called just to ask how she was doing.

"We started weaning Emma this morning," he said, breaking the strained silence. "I don't know if she'll be extubated today or tomorrow, but hopefully soon."

"That's wonderful news," she said, thrilled beyond belief that the baby was improving. "That must mean her lungs still look good."

"Clear as a bell," he said, with a hint of humor in his voice. He was so attractive when he smiled although really he didn't smile often enough. "We caught the aspiration quickly enough to prevent pneumonia."

"I'm so glad." Cassie imagined how great it would be once Emma's breathing tube was removed and she could finally hold the baby in her arms. Even though she was off today, she was tempted to go in just to hold Emma.

"Did you sign up for the foster-care classes?" he asked.

"Yes, the first class is Thursday and thankfully I'm off work, so that's good. I was about to sign up for the other classes, too, but Gloria called to let me know that they're warming Trey up today. They put him on the hypothermia protocol yesterday after he got up to the ICU to prevent his brain from swelling."

"I know. I checked on him late last night, too," Ryan admitted. "Once he's warmed up, they'll ease off on the sedation to see if he'll wake up."

She was tempted to ask him why he cared so much about Trey's overdose, but she doubted he'd tell her over the phone something he wouldn't tell her in person.

Besides, she wasn't going to dwell on the details regarding his personal life, right? Right.

"Will you let me know if Emma gets extubated?" she asked, changing the focus of the conversation back to the baby.

"Absolutely. Are you free for dinner?" he asked. "There's a great Italian place overlooking Lake Michigan. We won't see the sunset since the lake is obviously in the east, but it's still an amazing view."

She pulled her phone away from her ear and stared at it in confusion. Why was he asking her out? Especially after the way he'd pulled away after their kiss?

Despite how badly she wanted to say yes, she forced herself to rein in her emotions. "I don't think so," she said. "You're the one who told me that you weren't ready for a relationship."

"I know, but I can't stop thinking about you, Cassandra," he admitted in a low, gravelly tone that sent shivers of awareness dancing down her spine. "For the first time since Victoria died, I feel alive. And I'm pretty sure it's because of you."

Her heart squeezed in her chest and she drew in a harsh breath. She knew she should refuse, if for no other reason than to protect her heart, but at the same time it was difficult to ignore his request. Did she dare believe that something more permanent might grow between them? Would her being a foster mother be enough for him someday? Or would he want children of his own?

"Cassie, please," he said, when she didn't answer. "Say you'll have dinner with me?"

Her heart spoke before her brain could overrule her snap decision. "Yes, Ryan," she said huskily. "I'd be happy to have dinner with you."

"Thanks," he murmured. "I'd like to bring the convertible since the weather is nice."

"I'd like that," she agreed, ignoring the tiny niggle of doubt that this was a good decision.

"Sounds good. I'll pick you up at seven o'clock."

"All right. See you then." Cassie disconnected and then buried her face in her hands.

What was she doing? Going out with Ryan again was not part of her plan. Hadn't she told herself not to risk getting emotionally involved with him?

Yes, but obviously she was too late.

She was already emotionally involved with Ryan, whether she wanted to be or not.

She cared about him, far too much.

Ryan knew he was grinning like a fool when he walked back into the NNICU to check on Emma's condition, but he didn't care if the staff stared at him.

Cassie was giving him another chance. Only this time he had to figure out a way not to blow it.

A feat easier said than done.

"She's tolerating the new vent settings very well," Claire said when he approached Emma's warmer. The speculation in the nurse's gaze made him wonder if the rumors had already started about him seeing Cassie.

Oddly enough, the idea didn't bring on a wave of desperate panic the way it had after the Shana fiasco.

"I'm glad to hear it," he said, glancing down at the arterial blood gas results Claire had given him. "Follow the weaning pattern for the rest of the day, but call me before you leave for the day."

"Okay," Claire agreed. "No big plans today?"

She was fishing for information, but instead of becoming annoyed he simply smiled. "Talk to you later."

He headed home, maintaining his good mood, happiness all but oozing from his pores. Knowing that he would see Cassie later that evening was enough to keep him motivated.

Because he hadn't lied to her about the effect she had

on him. He felt alive, and couldn't help wondering if that small frozen part of his heart was beginning to thaw.

Because of her. And Emma, too.

He pulled into the driveway, glad to see the Realtor had already posted a For Sale sign in his front yard. He knew better than to get his hopes up that he'd manage to sell the albatross quickly, but his good mood refused to be dampened.

For months now he'd put off the job of packing up the things he didn't need. Victoria's family had taken her things, along with the baby furniture, a long time ago, so only his belongings were left.

Way more things that one man needed, that was for sure.

Ryan forced himself to head to the gym before tackling the job of packing up the items he didn't need. The Realtor, Andrea, told him the less clutter in his house, the better it would look to prospective buyers.

He had no reason not to believe her.

A few hours later, after he'd packed four large boxes, his phone rang. He picked it up, recognizing Trammel's number.

"This is Ryan Murphy," he said by way of greeting.

"Dr. Murphy, did you leave a message asking me to call?" Trammel asked.

"Yes, I did," Ryan admitted. Holding the phone to his ear, he crossed the kitchen for the list he'd made earlier. "I did a search on physicians named Oliver Stevenson in neighboring states. It's possible one of their DEA numbers matches the one used to fill the prescriptions."

"Just the neighboring states?" Trammel asked dryly. "I'm surprised you didn't check all fifty."

"I will if you'd like," Ryan offered, even though he

knew the detective was kidding. Trammel didn't understand how badly he wanted to find the identity of the person who was behind these fake scripts.

"I'll take this list for now," Trammel said, "but I have to be honest—it's possible the doctor could be from anywhere."

Trammel wasn't telling him anything he hadn't already considered himself. But they had to start somewhere and it made sense that the DEA number was from a physician close by, rather than on the other side of the country.

"I'll scan the list and email it to you," Ryan said. "Give me your email address."

Trammel rattled it off for him, while he scribbled the information on a scrap piece of paper.

"I'll let you know if anything pops from the list," Detective Trammel said.

Ryan knew that Trammel was making an effort to include him in as much of the investigation as possible and he was deeply grateful. "I appreciate that, Detective."

"Just remember to leave the investigating to me," Trammel added wryly.

He couldn't help but grin. "I'll try."

After disconnecting from the call, Ryan decided to go through his bedroom closet before ending his packing for the day. He grimaced when he saw the number of suits he had, along with all the golf pants and shirts.

He hadn't hit a single golf ball since Victoria's death. And, truthfully, he didn't miss it. Golf was part of the life he'd wanted nothing more to do with after losing his unborn son. So he started with those items first, putting them in a bag that he'd give to the Salvation Army.

As he worked, a small brown folder fell out from one

of the pockets of his golf pants. He went still, realizing what the small envelope contained.

A copy of the sonogram photo of his unborn son.

His fingers shook a bit as he picked it up and opened the metal clasp. He pulled out the small square of radiology film and held it up to the light.

The tiny body of his son was easy to see.

His throat tightened and the old familiar guilt squeezed his heart. His marriage to Victoria hadn't been great, but he'd wanted this baby so badly. It had been difficult to accept that his son hadn't been given a fair chance to live.

His heart squeezed in his chest, but for the first time in years he wasn't consumed with anger at the unfairness of it all—mad at Victoria for being selfish and at himself for being blind and stupid.

Instead, he grew more determined than ever to make sure Emma was provided the chance to grow and thrive in a way his son hadn't been able to.

Cassie vacillated between looking forward to dinner with Ryan and wondering if she should cancel.

She'd spent the morning signing up for as many foster-care classes as she could with her current work schedule. When she was finished with that, she wrote down the dates and times of the other classes and headed to Cedar Bluff Hospital to talk to her boss.

There had to be a way to switch shifts with someone or to take vacation time. As a last resort, she could take a personal unpaid leave of absence, but even that would have to be approved by her boss and by Human Resources.

When she arrived, Michelle, the nurse manager

for the neonatal ICU, was tied up in a meeting, so she headed down to the ICU to check on Gloria.

"How's Trey?" she asked.

"Oh, Cass, he's starting to wake up," Gloria said, hope shining from her eyes. "He's moving all his extremities but isn't quite following commands yet."

"Give him time, Gloria," she urged, giving her friend a hug. "I have a good feeling about this."

"Me, too," Gloria admitted. "Last night was the longest night of my life, but today things are looking up. If he begins to follow commands, I'll feel even better."

"He will." Cassie wouldn't allow her friend to worry about the worst-case scenario. "Do you mind if I sit here with you for a few minutes? I'm waiting for Michelle to come out of a meeting."

"No problem." Gloria dropped into the waiting room chair and Cassie sat down beside her. "Why do you need to talk to your boss?"

Cassie explained about how there were six foster-care classes that clashed with her schedule.

"I can't believe you're going to be a single mother," Gloria said, a tiny frown puckering her brow.

"You don't think it's a good idea," Cassie said, reading her body language. "But trust me, I know what I want."

"You'll be a great mother, Cass, it's just—don't you want to wait until you have a husband? Maybe give birth to a child of your own?"

Cassie took a deep breath. "I need surgery before I can even try to get pregnant again and even then there's a good chance I won't be able to carry a baby to term," she admitted, ignoring the way Ryan's face flashed into her mind at the thought of getting married again. "So, you see, this is the right thing to do. Emma needs me, Gloria, as much as I need her."

Gloria's expression softened. "I can tell you love her already, so if that's what you want to do, then any man who falls in love with you will just have to deal with it, right?"

An image of Ryan holding Daniel flashed in her mind. He obviously adored babies. Had admitted he wanted children of his own. But did that extend to fostering? She had no idea. Her phone vibrated. She'd turned off the ringer while in the hospital and recognized the hospital number. "Sorry, Gloria, I think this is Michelle."

"Go and meet with her. We'll chat later."

Cassie answered the phone. The unit clerk in the neonatal unit let her know that Michelle had returned. "Don't let her run off. I'll be right there."

She took the stairs up to the third floor, unwilling to wait for the elevator. Michelle was in her office and surprisingly supportive of the schedule changes Cassie needed.

Once she had everything set, Cassie hurried back home to sign up for the remaining classes. But this time, when she tried to register, the system spit back a message.

Your status as a potential foster parent has been temporarily suspended. Please make an appointment with our administrator as soon as possible.

Cassie stared at the message in horror. What was going on? She rummaged through her purse, looking for Mr. Davies's card for his number. She called and had to navigate through several auto voice-mail prompts before she was able to finally speak to a real person.

"My name is Cassandra Jordan and I've just been notified that my status as a potential foster parent has been temporarily suspended," she said with a hitch in her tone. She was trying very hard not to cry, hoping that this was just some horrible mistake.

"Oh, yes, I'm sorry, but that is correct," the woman said in a cheerful tone that made Cassie want to scream with frustration.

"Would you mind telling me why?" Cassie asked. "Is there some form I forgot to fill out? Or some piece of information you need to clear this up?"

"Well, it appears that you listed a single-bedroom apartment as your current residence," the woman said. "I'm afraid we prefer that our foster children are given the opportunity to have their own rooms. However, we can make exceptions. You need approval from Mr. Davies."

"Two bedrooms," Cassie repeated, trying to absorb the implications. "Okay, I can understand that and actually I have a message in to my landlord to inquire if a two-bedroom apartment is available. Could I talk to Mr. Davies? I'd like an exception if possible so I can continue the process."

"I'm sorry, Mr. Davies is out of town for the rest of the week. He won't be back until next Monday. But I'll let him know that you called."

A week? But the classes started in three days! Cassie felt her phone slip from her fingers and crash to the table.

What if she lost the chance to be Emma's foster

mother because of this delay? Especially since Emma was getting better.

Her dream of being Emma's mother cracked and then shattered. Tears burned her eyes and she buried her face in her hands, succumbing to an overwhelming wave of despair.

CHAPTER TEN

RYAN COULDN'T BELIEVE how nervous he was as he approached Cassie's apartment door. He'd managed to catch someone coming out, so he hadn't needed to buzz her apartment to get in.

He straightened his shoulders and took a deep breath. He knew he was overreacting, that they were just having dinner, but at the same time he didn't want to mess up.

He rapped lightly on Cassie's door, resisting the urge to double-check that his shirt was tucked in. He'd dressed casually in a black pair of dress pants and a blue polo shirt. Maybe he should have chosen a button-down shirt and a tie?

The seconds ticked by with no response, so he frowned and knocked again, louder. After several more seconds the door opened a crack.

"I'm sorry, Ryan, but I'm not going to be able to keep our date," Cassie said in a low voice.

His instincts went on red alert, and not just because she was wearing cut-off jeans and T-shirt. Her face was blotchy and her eyes were swollen. "What's wrong? Have you been crying?"

She shook her head and sniffled loudly. "It's nothing, really. I'm sorry about dinner. I'll take a rain-check, okay?"

She stepped back and started to shut the door, but he quickly slapped his hand against it, holding firm. "Cassie, please, talk to me. I don't care about dinner, but it's obvious you're upset. Please, tell me what's wrong."

With a listless shrug she stepped back farther and let go of the door. He pushed it open wider and then stepped inside, closing the door behind him.

Cassie stood with her arms crossed defensively over her chest. "I'm sorry, I should have called before you made the trip out here," she said, avoiding his gaze.

"I don't care about our plans, but I do wish you'd called me earlier, because then I could have been here for you."

She shrugged again and turned away.

He could barely stand to see her so torn up like this. This couldn't be about Emma's condition since he knew the baby was doing all right. Claire had called to let him know that Emma had tolerated her weaning fairly well, but looked as if she was getting tired, so he'd decided to let her rest overnight and then work on weaning her again in the morning.

So what had happened to make Cassie cry?

"Please, tell me what happened. Didn't you get into the foster-care classes? Or did your boss refuse to work with your schedule?"

She bit her lower lip and then turned to face him. "I don't think I can take the classes until I speak with the administrator and he's out of the office until next week," she said bluntly, her eyes filling with tears. "Which means, I may not be approved in time to be there for Emma."

He couldn't help it, he crossed over and drew her against him in a reassuring hug. She seemed to resist for a moment but then buried her face against his chest.

"I'm so sorry," he murmured, thinking it wasn't fair that her world was on hold until some administrator came back from his vacation.

"I know I'm being ridiculous but I wanted so badly to be Emma's mother," she said, her voice muffled against his shirt. "I should just be happy that Emma will go to a good home, but I'm selfish, Ryan. I wanted her to be with me."

"Shh, Cassie, you're not selfish," he said, resting his cheek against her hair and smoothing his hand down her back. Even though he was all too aware of her curves pressed against him, he kept his touch gentle, reassuring. "It's clear you two belong together. I wish there was something I could do to help."

"Thanks, Ryan, but there isn't anything we can do until next week. Which will probably be too late." She drew back a little to look up into his eyes. "But it's nice to know you care enough to try."

He did care, far more than he should. He wanted to give Cassie everything and it was frustrating to have this issue outside his control. "Don't give up," he urged in a low voice. "You're already signed up for the first class this week anyway, right?" When she gave a hesitant nod, he continued, "Then go and we'll get this cleared up next week. It will all be fine, you'll see. Besides, it's clear to anyone with eyes in their head that you and Emma belong together."

Her tremulous smile tugged at his heart. "Sure, why not?" Then she tipped her head to the side, her gaze quizzical. "Do you really think we belong together?"

"Yes, I do," he said with conviction. "Not everyone has the mothering instincts that you do, Cassie. Every time I see you holding Emma, you take my breath away."

"Oh, Ryan," she murmured. "I think that's the nicest thing anyone has ever said to me. Thank you."

His heart twisted in his chest and for a moment he wanted to smack that cheating ex-husband of hers for hurting her. He lowered his head to kiss her cheek, but she surprised him by coming up on tiptoe to press her mouth against his.

He tried to offer comfort, but Cassie's lips teased his until he opened his mouth and deepened their kiss. The way she melted into his arms, molding herself against him, made tiny stars explode behind his eyes.

Nothing had ever felt so right as having Cassie in his arms. His body was on fire and soon the flames were so stoked he wasn't capable of thinking at all.

Cassie knew that she'd broken her no-kissing rule in a big way but couldn't seem to find the energy to pull away. Ryan had been there for her emotionally when she'd needed him most, far different than Evan had ever been.

And when he deepened the kiss, exploring her mouth so intently, she wrapped her arms around his neck and hung on as her knees threatened to buckle.

Every nerve in her body hummed with sizzling awareness and she returned his kiss, letting all the passion she'd once buried deep inside burst free.

This was what she'd been missing from her life. For the life of her, she couldn't remember why she'd felt the need to stay away from him. Not when being in his arms felt so right.

Ryan lifted his head, his blue eyes glittering down at her with fierce intensity. "Cassandra, you're so beautiful," he murmured. He pressed his lips against the curve of her jaw, and then trailed a path down the side of her neck, making her shiver with anticipation.

"You make me feel beautiful," she whispered, and then gasped when he pulled her closer and she could feel the hard ridge of his erection.

Need zinged through her bloodstream and she found herself squirming against him, desperate to get closer still. His musky scent went straight to her head, more potent than a shot of liquor. What was Ryan doing to her? She'd never felt like this before.

"Cassandra," he murmured in a deep voice tinged with the same desperation she felt. "If you don't want to do this, tell me now."

By *this*, she knew he meant making love.

She hadn't been intimate with a man in well over a year and a half. In fact, she'd had no trouble staying celibate.

Until now.

"I do want this, Ryan," she said, drowning in his fierce blue eyes. "I want you."

A smile tugged at the corner of his mouth. "Thank God," he muttered, covering her mouth in another searing kiss. When he lifted his head to breathe, he added, "I'm glad to know I'm not in this alone."

The hint of vulnerability in his tone made her fall even more completely under his spell. She kissed the side of his neck, and then let out a squeal when he swept her legs out from under her.

He carried her into her bedroom before gently setting her on her feet. Before she could blink, he'd stripped off his shirt and then reached for the hem of her T-shirt.

She wished she'd dressed nicer for him, but as he peeled her shirt up and over her head, his gaze feasting on her breasts encased in a pink lacy bra, she realized it didn't matter. His fingers found the button on her ragged shorts and, with deft movements, he pushed them down to the floor so she could step out of them.

She fumbled with his belt and in a flash of impatience he whipped it off and took off his slacks. He wore black boxers that barely covered his arousal and for the first time since he'd kissed her she felt a sliver of unease.

Not for what they were about to do but whether or not she'd live up to his expectations.

Sex with her ex hadn't exactly been earth-shattering.

"Cassie, tell me what's going on in your head," Ryan urged, drawing her close. "Is something wrong? Have you changed your mind?"

She shoved away thoughts of her ex with an effort. "I haven't been with a man in a long time," she confessed. "I'm afraid of disappointing you."

"Trust me, there's no possible way in the world you could disappoint me. You're the warmth I desperately need," he murmured, his gaze serious. "And it's been a long time for me, too." He cupped her face in his hands and kissed her reverently and then with frank desire. He stripped away her bra and panties and gently drew her toward the bed.

She ran her hands over his taut muscles, reveling in the light dusting of hair sprinkled across his chest. He lowered his head to her breasts, lavishing his attention on one nipple and then the other, intensifying the ache between her legs to the point she wasn't sure she could stand the sensual torture much longer.

"Please," she begged, wrapping her legs around his waist. "Now. I want you inside me now!"

Ryan suckled her taut nipple even as he ran his hand down her abdomen, probing gently between her legs.

"Please," she said again, gasping as pleasure washed over her when he stroked his finger over her clit.

"You're so hot and ready for me," he murmured, drawing back to stare at her flushed body. She reached up for him, but he was busy tearing open a small foil packet.

She wanted to protest, even though she knew how foolish that would be. So she watched as he slid the condom on and then lifted her hips in a silent invitation.

He spread her legs wider and guided himself toward her moist entrance. She expected discomfort, but, surprisingly, there wasn't any pain as he thrust deep.

Ryan let out a low groan and began to move back and forth in gentle thrusts that soon became more and more urgent.

"Yes," she whispered, straining against him. "Oh, yes."

"Cassandra…" His voice broke on her name as he quickened his pace, gathering her even more tightly against him. "Come with me," he begged, before lowering his mouth to capture hers in a deep kiss.

A kaleidoscope of color burst behind her eyes as wave after wave of pleasure shuddered through her. His big body shook against hers, too, and she surrendered to him, reveling in the intensity of the moment, realizing that nothing had ever felt so right.

* * *

Ryan shifted onto his back, drawing Cassie over his chest and anchoring her with an arm across her waist, trying to drag badly needed oxygen into his lungs.

Incredible. Making love with Cassie had been absolutely incredible.

His heart thudded in his chest, slowly returning to a normal rhythm. Cassie's body lay sated and limp against him and he summoned the energy to trail his hand over her satiny-smooth skin. He couldn't help but smile, wishing they could stay like this forever.

"Wow," she murmured.

"Yeah, wow," he agreed.

She snuggled against him and amazingly he felt the stirring of desire. Apparently he hadn't had enough of Cassie.

Would he ever get enough of her?

A fissure of panic skated down his spine. He tried to ignore it, but it wasn't easy. Being with Cassie had been amazing.

Yet she deserved so much more than a quick release.

He told himself this wasn't anything like what he'd had with Shana, but the old self-doubts came marching back.

"Thanks for not being upset with me," she said, craning her neck to look up at him.

He frowned. "Upset? About this? No way."

She laughed and shook her head. "About falling apart and completely forgetting about our dinner date."

He wasn't at all angry with her about that. He knew how much being a foster parent for Emma meant to her.

"Cassie, it's going to be all right, you'll see." He kissed the top of her head, liking the way he could feel her smile against his chest. "And who knows, you might have children of your own someday."

There was a long pause and he sensed there was something he'd said wrong, but before he could try to backtrack his phone jangled, interrupting the moment.

He groaned inwardly, tempted to ignore it. But what if the call was from the hospital? Cassie must have had the same thought because she pulled away, wrapping the sheet around her as she moved to the side of the bed, giving him plenty of room to get up.

He didn't want to leave her, but the phone kept ringing so he rolled off the bed and knelt next to his discarded clothes, searching for the stupid thing.

When he saw Detective Trammel's number, his pulse jumped. "This is Ryan Murphy," he said.

"Dr. Murphy, I wanted to tell you we got a hit on one of the names you gave us," Trammel said, getting straight to the point. "The DEA number of Oliver Stevenson from Chicago, Illinois matches the one used on the prescription used by Trey Reynolds."

"It does?" Ryan sank down on the edge of Cassie's bed, uncaring that he was still stark naked. He'd been waiting so long for a clue related to Victoria's death.

And now they finally had one.

"Where's Stevenson's office?" Ryan demanded. "We need to get there before he closes up his pill shop and moves on."

"Whoa, there, not so fast," Trammel interrupted. "You aren't doing anything, understand? So help me, Murphy, if you interfere with my investigation, I'll cut you out of the information loop so fast your head will spin."

Ryan bit back a scathing retort, unwilling to make Trammel any angrier than he already was. He was fortunate that the detective even bothered to keep him abreast of the investigation at all, and he knew the older man wouldn't hesitate to follow through on his threat.

"I won't interfere with your investigation," Ryan said, forcing the words past his tight throat. He glanced over to find Cassie's intense gaze boring into his, unspoken questions reflected in her eyes, and his stomach dropped to the soles of his feet. He'd been so glad to hear from the detective that he'd forgotten about the fact that Cassie was listening to him. "Thanks for calling, Detective."

"You're welcome," Trammel said grudgingly.

Ryan disconnected from the call and tossed his phone on the bed.

"Detective? What was that about?" she asked, holding the sheet protectively against her chest. "Why would you interfere with a police investigation?"

Ryan grimaced, knowing it was well past time to tell her the truth. He pulled on his boxers, wishing he'd let Trammel's call go to his voice mail.

"Ryan?"

He let out a heavy breath. "Remember when I told you I had a personal interest in overdose cases?"

She nodded, taking a step backward as if needing to put more space between them. He wanted to cross over to her and pull her into his arms, but forced himself to stay where he was.

"I was interested in what happened to Gloria's brother Trey because my wife died of a narcotic overdose."

Cassie put her hand to her chest, her gaze full of compassion. "Accidental? Or on purpose?" she asked.

He raked his fingers through his hair, wishing he'd picked a better time to have this conversation. Talk about a buzzkill. "Accidental, according to the medical examiner. And I don't think Victoria would have taken her own life."

"Oh, Ryan, that must have been horrible for you." Her brown eyes were full of compassion, an emotion he didn't deserve.

"Don't," he said harshly, grabbing his pants and stepping into them. "You don't understand. It doesn't matter what the ME decided, because her death was completely my fault."

She stared at him for a long moment. "I don't understand," she whispered.

He shook his head, knowing he should tell her the rest but unable to get the words past his throat.

He never talked about Victoria or the loss of his unborn son. Especially not to other women. Even his buddy Simon only knew the watered-down version.

He couldn't do it.

"I have to go." Ryan knew that if he didn't leave now he'd tell her everything, only to see something worse than compassion in Cassie's eyes.

Condemnation. For the role he'd played in his son's death.

She stared at him without saying a word as he finished getting dressed. "Take care," he said, before walking out of the bedroom door.

He didn't hear a response, not that he blamed her. After all, he'd ruined their perfect evening.

And she didn't even know the worst about him yet.

Walking away wasn't easy. He cared about Cassie, too much. And as he left he realized that, despite everything, the small part of his heart that he'd thought frozen was aching painfully now.

CHAPTER ELEVEN

CASSIE SPENT A horribly restless night on her sofa, before dragging herself upright the moment the sun came up over the horizon.

So much had happened last night and she was still struggling to understand exactly why things had deteriorated so quickly after the most incredible lovemaking she'd ever experienced in her entire life. She'd felt so close to Ryan, had been about to confide about her miscarriages and her inability to have children—until his phone had rung. At first she'd thought it was the hospital, but had then realized he'd been talking to the detective who was investigating Trey's overdose.

She'd felt terrible for him, knowing that he'd lost his wife to a narcotic overdose. No wonder he'd gone flying down to the ER when he'd heard about Trey. His actions now made perfect sense.

He blamed himself, yet wouldn't tell her why.

Knowing he couldn't confide in her made her wonder if he was holding back because he knew the truth was something she might not be able to handle.

Nausea swirled in her belly. Maybe it was better that she hadn't confided her deepest secret. After watching him with Daniel and hearing him admit that he wanted kids someday, she knew that her medical issues would be a stumbling block. Oh, sure, he might convince himself that it didn't matter until at some point he'd keenly regret not being able to father his own child.

She never should have made love with him, even though that intimacy had only emphasized how deeply she cared about him. Clearly he had the power to hurt her far worse than Evan ever had.

The sick feeling in her stomach grew worse, but she did her best to ignore it. She forced herself to make a slice of toast, hoping the bit of food would help make her feel better.

She wasn't normally the type to skip meals, but she hadn't eaten anything for dinner last night and now could barely face breakfast. This was ridiculous; it wasn't as if anyone had died. Okay, maybe she'd jumped the gun by making love with Ryan when there was so much they obviously didn't know about each other, but at least Emma was getting better.

She needed to snap out of it, pull herself together.

She had plenty of things she could do to take her mind off her problems. It wasn't like her to wallow in self-pity so she forced herself to finish her toast, trying not to think about how much the bread tasted like cardboard. At least the nauseous feeling in her stomach subsided a bit.

After taking a shower, she felt a little more human, enough to face the day, anyway. She needed to do something productive to fill the hours between now and the start of her shift at three o'clock that afternoon.

She decided to call the apartment manager again and thankfully this time he answered. "Hey, Cassie, sorry I didn't get back to you yesterday."

"That's okay. Do you have a two-bedroom apartment available?"

"Not right now. I have several one bedrooms open, but for some reason the two-bedroom apartments go fast. I'll know more in a few months."

A few months? She tried not to succumb to a deep stab of disappointment. "Will you please let me know as soon as a two-bedroom unit becomes available?"

"Sure thing," he promised.

She set her phone aside, wishing there was more she could do to break down the obstacles standing between her and Emma. When her phone rang a short time later she thought for sure it was Ryan, calling to apologize. But her bubble of hope deflated, followed by a twinge of guilt, when she recognized Gloria's number on the screen.

"Hi, Gloria, how is Trey doing?" she said.

"Trey woke up this morning, Cass. He woke up!" Her friend's enthusiasm was contagious.

"Oh, Gloria, that's wonderful news! I'm so happy for you and your family."

"I'm ecstatic, too, believe me. I know Detective Trammel will want to talk to him about where he got the prescription, but that's the least of our worries now. No matter what happens, he'll be fine."

"I know what you mean," Cassie said with heartfelt sympathy. She decided not to mention Ryan's participation in Trey's prescription investigation. "Getting into a little trouble isn't anything compared with almost dying."

"Would you be willing to meet me for lunch?" Gloria asked. "I'm going to head home to shower and change. I'm too keyed up to sleep."

"Of course I'll have lunch with you," Cassie agreed. "Do you want me to come to your apartment? We can walk to the Sunshine Café, it's not too far. We can sit outside and enjoy the day."

"Perfect," Gloria said. "How about you head over here in about an hour?"

"Sure, see you then," she agreed. Since she had an hour to kill, she opened her notebook computer and began searching for houses in the Cedar Bluff area. Most of the homes were well beyond her price range, making her wince. Borrowing against her retirement fund wasn't going to help if she couldn't afford to make the monthly mortgage payments.

She regretted now that she'd refused the small settlement Evan had tried to give her during their divorce. Her lawyer tried to tell her to take the money, but she'd only taken enough to cover the legal fees and nothing more.

Thrusting the useless wish aside, she stumbled on a small townhouse that was for sale at a reasonable price. She stared at the property, her heart pounding with excitement. This could be the break she'd been waiting for.

She quickly jotted down the address, determined to swing by the place on her way to work. Then she scrolled down to the mortgage calculator, entering round numbers for an estimate of what she'd need to buy the place.

The projected mortgage plus property taxes was only about two hundred more than what she was paying in rent now.

She could do this. She really might be able to do this!

Cassie called the real estate agent listed on the website and left a message, stating she wanted to see the property as soon as possible. Then she clicked through the photos again, thinking that the townhouse was the perfect place for her and Emma.

And she had no doubt she'd be able to convince Mr. Davies to make an exception for her.

As she headed over to Gloria's building, she battled the need to call Ryan to share her good news.

But she didn't.

The excitement of being Emma's foster mother paled when she realized just how much she'd come to depend on Ryan's emotional support.

And how much she missed his support now that it was gone.

Ryan finished packing the last box in the back of his buddy's pickup truck, swiping a hand over his forehead in relief. Once this load had been hauled away, he'd be one step closer to getting rid of the albatross around his neck.

Simon came around the pickup to meet Ryan. "Is that everything?"

"Yes. Are you sure you don't mind taking it for me? I'd be happy to make the run over there myself."

"No problem." Simon waved away his offer. "Let me know if you need anything else."

"I don't, unless you know someone who wants to buy this place," he said wryly.

Simon made a face. "Sorry, man, but Holly's pregnant again and this place isn't exactly child-friendly."

Ryan couldn't blame his buddy considering they already had a three-year-old son who was constantly getting into everything. "Never mind. Thanks again."

"Okay, see you later."

Ryan watched as Simon jumped into the cab of the pickup truck, which slowly lumbered away.

Finishing up with the house had kept his mind busy, but now that he had the rest of the day stretching before him, thoughts of Cassie came flooding back. He'd come close to calling her at least a dozen times that morning, and the urge to do so again was strong.

He wanted to apologize for walking away, although at the same time he knew he'd wouldn't be able to live with himself until he'd told her the truth. The entire truth.

When had he become so dependent on Cassie to get through the day?

Since Emma. The safe-haven baby had been the catalyst to draw them together.

But his past was keeping them apart.

Trammel had called to let him know that they were still trying to track down the Oliver Stevenson from Illinois. Interestingly enough, the address listed on Trey's oxycodone prescription was also an abandoned office building in yet another strip mall just over the Wisconsin/Illinois border. Ryan was depressed that they'd hit another dead end.

Thankfully Trammel was like a dog with a bone, determined to get to the bottom of where exactly the prescription had come from.

Since Trammel didn't need his help, his thoughts swirled back to Cassie. The memory of their lovemaking kept looping over and over again in his mind, making him want nothing more than to have her again. He knew she'd been with him, too, begging for him to take her. Their lovemaking had been an experience that had pretty much blown him away.

Stop it, he told himself firmly. No matter how much he wanted Cassie, he'd been the one to walk away. He'd taken the easy way out, too cowardly to tell her the truth.

Would she give him a second chance? Even though he didn't deserve it?

And what if her feelings changed once she knew the real him?

Ryan's head pounded with indecision. He showered, shaved and changed his clothes, before reaching for his phone. They needed to be able to work together so he sucked in a deep breath and called Cassie. When she didn't answer, he decided against leaving a voice mail message.

Really, it would be better to talk to her in person. Without giving himself a chance to think too much, he headed out to the convertible.

With any luck, she'd be at her apartment.

But, of course, she didn't answer the door. Dejected, he turned away, wondering if she was avoiding him.

He didn't want to go back home, and since it was close to lunchtime he decided to stop and grab something to eat. Driving past the Sunshine Café, he did a double take when he saw Cassie standing next to Gloria as they waited for a table to be cleared. She looked happy, even laughing at something Gloria had said.

His stomach clenched painfully as he realized Cassie was doing fine without him. She wasn't upset about the way he'd left last night after all.

He forced himself to face the truth. That she might not be as emotionally involved in what had transpired between them.

Not the same way he'd been.

* * *

Cassie caught a glimpse of Ryan's red convertible, but before she could move, either toward him or away from him, he was gone.

There was no reason to be disappointed. He'd walked away last night and clearly didn't plan to apologize anytime soon.

And maybe putting distance between them was for the best.

While she and Gloria waited for their table to be cleared, she subtly checked her phone, hoping the real estate agent who had listed the townhouse had called her back.

Andrea Langley hadn't responded, but Cassie did find a missed call from Ryan.

She stared at the screen in shock. And despite her earlier vow to stay away from him, a warm glow spread through her at the fact that he'd tried to get in touch with her.

Maybe he did want to apologize after all. And if she was honest, she'd admit that Ryan wasn't the only one with secrets. Maybe they needed to clear the air between them once and for all.

"Hello, Cass, are you listening?" Gloria said in exasperation.

"What? Oh, sorry. What did you say?"

Gloria rolled her eyes. "I asked how our safe-haven baby was doing."

"She's had a rough couple of days, but she's doing better," Cassie said. She leaned forward and propped her elbows on the table. "Remember I told you how I'm trying to become a foster parent? Turns out I need a two-bedroom place or to get special approval from the administrator, first."

Gloria's jaw dropped open. "You're kidding."

"Nope, and, worse, the administrator is out of the office until next week. There aren't any two-bedroom apartments open at our place, so I've been scouring websites for potential houses. Right now, there isn't much out there that I can afford."

"Maybe you should hold off, Cass," Gloria said, her eyes reflecting her concern. "Seems drastic to do all this when you don't know for sure you'll even have the chance to take care of Emma."

Cassie frowned, dejected by her friend's doom-and-gloom attitude. "Important things are never easy," she said, glancing down at her menu. Ironically, her appetite had returned with a vengeance. "Hmm, the grilled chicken sandwich looks awesome."

"It sure does. I should have a salad, but what the heck. Let's go for it." Gloria shoved her menu aside, as if just looking at it would change her mind.

"Okay. And I can vouch for the homemade chips, they're amazing."

"Really?" Gloria raised a brow. "I didn't realize you've eaten here before."

Cassie blushed, remembering the burger she'd had with Ryan. "Just once," she said. "Although I'm not sure why we haven't come here more often. This café is close enough to our apartment building."

Her phone rang and she pulled it out of her lap, her heart racing when she recognized the number of the Realtor. "Sorry, Gloria, I have to take this," she said hastily.

"Hello, this is Cassandra Jordan," she answered, rising to her feet and moving off to the side so she wouldn't bother anyone.

"Andrea Langley. I understand you're interested in seeing the townhouse on Lavender Drive?"

"Yes, I am," Cassie said firmly. "Can we set up a time to view it as soon as possible?"

"Yes. How about three o'clock this afternoon?"

Cassie's heart sank. "I start work at three. Could we meet at two instead?"

"Sure. I'll switch things around so I can meet you there at two o'clock."

"Great, thanks." Cassie disconnected from the call, tempted to do another little happy dance.

She managed to restrain herself, but as she turned back toward Gloria she caught a glimpse of Lydia, the cane lady.

It was starting to be uncanny the way she kept bumping into this woman, and Cassie headed over with steely determination.

"Hello, Ms. Lydia. How are you doing this afternoon?"

"Oh, I'm fine, just fine." Lydia looked flustered, although Cassie wasn't sure why. This woman seemed to be following her, not the other way around.

And suddenly Cassie was tired of playing games.

"Do you want an update on Emma's condition?" she asked bluntly. "Because I know you're related to that baby in some way."

Lydia opened her mouth and then closed it again without saying anything. She looked down at her cane and then dragged her gaze back up to meet Cassie's. "I have rheumatoid arthritis, and my doctor says that my physical condition is going to deteriorate rapidly over the next year or two."

Cassie wasn't sure why this poor woman was telling her this. "I'm sorry, that must have been very difficult to hear. Isn't there any treatment or medications available that might help?"

Lydia shrugged. "Steroids and anti-inflammatory medications, which I'm already taking. And physical therapy, which I attend three mornings a week."

"That's encouraging," Cassie said, sitting down in the empty chair beside Lydia. "I've heard physical therapy can work wonders."

Lydia scowled down at her tea. "I haven't been impressed, considering I'm going to have to give up my cane for a walker soon. I've already fallen once. If I have another fall, I'm stuck with the stupid walker."

"I'm sorry," Cassie said helplessly. She truly did feel bad for this woman. She couldn't imagine what it must be like to know what physical limitations one was facing.

"None of that is the point," Lydia said in a feisty tone. Cassie had to give the woman credit for not letting her bleak prognosis get her down. "You asked me before if I knew Emma's mother, and I lied to you. I do know her. Emma's mother is my niece. My sister died several years ago and Avery—well, let's just say she's made a lot of bad decisions over the past few years."

Cassie didn't interrupt, silently encouraging the woman to talk.

"You see, Avery delivered in the hospital, but then left the very next day, without any support other than her boyfriend. And then she drove up here to ask for my help in raising the baby. But she also made it clear she wasn't going to stick around." Lydia's anguish was etched on her features. "It almost killed me, but as much as I wanted to take care of little Emma, I'm not physically able to. So I encouraged Avery to drop her off at the hospital. Giving Emma up as a safe-haven baby was the only option."

Cassie reached over and took Lydia's hand in hers. "You and Avery made the right decision," she said softly. "Emma is going to be fine. The doctor is hoping to take her breathing tube out soon, maybe even today. She's going to find a home with a lucky family one day soon, I promise."

"Thank you," Lydia said, tears welling in her eyes. "Thank you for taking such good care of my great-niece."

Cassie battled tears, too. "I'm taking good care of Emma. In fact, I'm hoping to become her foster mother, so I can take care of her, forever."

Saying the words out loud made them seem all the more real. But she didn't regret telling Lydia her dream.

She hoped the news would give the older woman some peace.

CHAPTER TWELVE

RYAN HEADED DOWN the highway that hugged the coastline of Lake Michigan, trying to talk himself out of going back to the Sunshine Café, but it was no use. He couldn't find it in him to stay away.

He desperately wanted to talk to Cassie, to apologize for leaving. And to tell her the truth, so that she knew everything about him, once and for all.

He made a U-turn so he could head back to Cedar Bluff. Maybe Cassie had moved on. Maybe she didn't need him the way he needed her. Maybe he was only doing this for himself, but he knew he wouldn't be able to move forward until he'd apologized. He parked his car a couple of blocks down and walked along the café's outdoor seating area. When he caught sight of Cassie talking to Lydia, he quickened his pace.

"Take care, Ms. Lydia," Cassie said, rising to her feet. "Remember, you have my phone number now, so call if you need something."

"I will, dear, thank you."

He approached, glancing warily between them. It seemed as if their conversation was amicable, but what had changed? "Hi, Cassie. Is everything okay?"

Her smile didn't quite meet her eyes. "Absolutely.

Ms. Lydia, you remember Dr. Murphy? He's one of the doctors caring for Emma."

"Yes, of course. How are you, Dr. Murphy?" Lydia held out her hand to Ryan. "Forgive me for not standing up, but my old bones are a bit achy today."

"Please, sit and relax," Ryan said, raising a curious eyebrow toward Cassie. He couldn't imagine what had changed since the last time they'd tried to speak to the woman.

"Ms. Lydia was just telling me that she's Emma's great-aunt," Cassie said, answering his unspoken question. "Her niece, Avery, has had some trouble and it was Ms. Lydia who told her to bring Emma to the hospital as a safe-haven baby."

"I see," Ryan murmured, turning back toward Lydia. "That was a wonderful thing you and Avery did. Thank you so much for giving Emma a chance at a better life."

"I would have kept Emma myself if not for this stupid rheumatoid arthritis," Lydia said with real regret in her eyes. "But I'm glad to hear Emma is doing okay. I've been so worried about the baby."

Ryan suspected Lydia knew more about Avery's history and he took the seat next to the older woman, choosing his words carefully. "I believe your niece might have a prescription drug addiction," he said, keeping his tone gentle. "I know you don't want her to get into any trouble, but at the same time it's important that Avery gets help before something bad happens to her."

Lydia pursed her lips for a moment and then nodded. "Yes, I know. I'm doing my best, but she's been running wild since my sister passed away. Unfortunately, Avery was in the car crash that killed my sister and she's has been suffering terrible back pain ever since. You're right about the prescription drugs, that's the reason she didn't stay very long in the hospital. But I'm not sure how to get her off them. Especially when she refuses to stay here and live with me. Apparently, she'd rather shack up with that worthless boyfriend of hers."

Knowing his instincts were right didn't make him feel any better. Helping people with addictions wasn't easy. Would he have been able to help Victoria if he'd known the truth? He wasn't sure. "I know it's hard, but when you do see her, please keep encouraging her to get help."

The older woman flashed him a tremulous smile. "I will."

Ryan carefully shook her hand and then stood up and followed Cassie back to the table where Gloria was waiting rather impatiently.

"Sorry about that, Gloria," Cassie said, as she took her seat. "I didn't mean to leave you here alone."

Gloria shrugged and put her phone away. She glanced up at Ryan. "Hi, Dr. Ryan. Do you want to join us?" she offered.

He absolutely did, but he glanced at Cassie, trying to read the impassive expression on her face. He sensed she wasn't thrilled to have him there, but at the same time he didn't want to leave without talking to her.

Although he'd rather not bare his soul in front of Gloria.

"I don't want to intrude. I'll sit somewhere else, but I would like to talk to you, Cassie. Maybe we could talk after you've finished your lunch?"

Cassie hesitated. "I may not have time," she said slowly. "I have an appointment at two o'clock."

Gloria seemed impervious to the tension between them. "It's silly of you to sit somewhere else. Cass, you don't mind if he joins us, do you?"

"No, of course not." Finally she met his gaze with a weak smile. "We've already placed our order so you may need to flag down the server."

Since she didn't seem too upset with him, he pulled out one of the empty chairs and sat down. He was hungry but was willing to forgo eating if it meant getting a chance to talk to Cassie. "Thank you," he murmured.

"Cass, what's your two o'clock appointment?" Gloria asked, taking a sip of her lemonade.

Cassie shrugged but he noticed that there was an excited glint in her eyes. "I found a townhouse for sale that happens to be close to my budget. I'm meeting the Realtor there this afternoon."

Ryan glanced at her in surprise. "Really?"

She nodded. "There aren't any two-bedroom units available so this is my best chance of getting Mr. Davies's approval to keep moving forward with the fostering process."

Was this why she'd looked so happy? Was it possible she didn't hate him for the way he left her so abruptly last night? "I'm glad to hear it. I could tag along if you like. I might be able to spot any problem areas."

She hesitated again, and he mentally kicked himself for pushing so hard. "I guess that would work." She surprised him by agreeing. "I don't know much about buying a house and need all the help I can get."

He was ridiculously pleased that she'd agreed to let him come along. "Thanks," he murmured.

Gloria cleared her throat loudly. "Do you two want

me to leave?" she asked. "It seems like you have a lot to discuss."

"No, of course not," he said, wincing a little at the fact that he'd made Gloria feel like a third wheel. "Let me know when you spot the server. I wouldn't mind having another one of their burgers. The last one I had was excellent."

Gloria snickered and raised an eyebrow toward Cassie, who blushed and stared down at her plate for a long moment.

He didn't understand the private joke but kept the conversation casual as the two women enjoyed their meal. Gloria updated him on her brother's progress and he was relieved to hear Trey had woken up and seemed to be doing okay. The server was so busy he didn't bother asking for a burger. Cassie insisted he share part of her lunch, so he helped himself to the smaller half of her sandwich and a handful of chips.

When the server returned with the bill, he quickly nabbed it and pulled out his wallet, ignoring Gloria and Cassie's loud protests.

"You had hardly anything to eat," Cassie said with exasperation. "Why should you pay?"

"Because I'm the one who interrupted your meal, forcing you to give up half your sandwich." He quickly stuffed cash into the plastic billfold and handed it back to the server. "Trust me, this is the least I can do."

Cassie sighed but didn't say anything more as she rose to her feet. He stood and followed her, longing for the easy camaraderie they'd once shared.

"I have a few errands to run," Gloria said. "I'll talk to you later, Cass, okay?"

"Sure. I'll check in on Trey during my dinner break," Cassie promised.

Ryan was grateful that Gloria had taken it upon herself to leave them alone. He felt a little guilty for interrupting their girl time, but thankfully Cassie didn't seem to mind.

"We have thirty minutes until we need to meet your Realtor," he said. "Would you like to take a drive in the convertible?"

She shook her head. "No, as much as I love your convertible, I need to stop by my apartment so I can pick up my scrubs and my stethoscope. I plan to head to work as soon as we're finished at the townhouse."

"No problem." He wondered if she regretted inviting him to go along. "I'll drive you over."

Stopping at Cassie's apartment didn't take long. When she came back out to his car with her bag over her shoulder, he wanted nothing more than to pull her close and kiss her.

But he forced himself to concentrate on telling her the truth first. "Cassie, I owe you an apology," he began, but she shook her head.

"Actually, there's no need for you to apologize. I have something I need to tell you," she said, cutting him off. "I think you should know why having Emma is so important to me."

He nodded, waiting for her to slide into the passenger seat of his convertible. "Okay."

She took a deep breath and let it out slowly. "I told you that my ex-husband cheated on me, but I didn't tell you everything."

He was surprised that she'd kept something back from him, too, although the tortured expression in her eyes didn't make him feel any better. "I'm listening," he encouraged.

"I suffered two miscarriages," she admitted. "Both at about twenty weeks' gestation."

His heart twisted in his chest. One was bad enough, but two? "I'm so sorry," he murmured.

"The worst part was that I had to be in the hospital after the second miscarriage because I wouldn't stop bleeding." Cassie turned in her seat to face him. "I heard my husband on the phone with his lover, telling her how glad he was that I'd lost the baby because now getting a divorce would be easier."

He curled his fingers into fists, wishing he could punch her ex right between the eyes. "I can't imagine how awful that must have been."

She dropped her gaze again. "I was getting ready to be taken into surgery for a D&C and told Evan to get out. I practically screamed at him that I wouldn't contest his stinking divorce."

Ryan wanted to pull her into his arms, and he must have reached toward her because she held up a hand.

"There's more. After surgery, the doctor told me that there was something wrong with my uterus, which was why I'd had the two miscarriages. There was some sort of tissue barrier making it smaller than normal. He told me that I needed to have another surgery before even trying to get pregnant again. And even then, the scar tissue might be too much to overcome."

"Cassie, I'm so sorry," he said tucking a strand of her dark hair behind her ear. "I wish there was something I could do to make you feel better."

Her attempt at a smile was pathetic. "Thanks, but there isn't anything you can do, although I appreciate your support. This is my burden to bear. I've always dreamed of having a family of my own, which is probably why I rushed into marriage with Evan."

"Just so you know, that loser is not worth a single tear," Ryan told her.

This time her smile looked real. "Thanks. I just wanted you to know that my chances of having a baby of my own are probably less than thirty percent. So now you know why I'm such an emotional wreck about being able to be a foster mother to Emma. And why this townhouse is so important to me."

"I do understand," he said slowly. "But, Cassie, you have to know that there are so many options available these days. The strides in reproductive medicine have been amazing. Even if you can't have children of your own, you can still have the family you've always dreamed of."

"Maybe," she admitted, although she looked far from convinced.

Ryan's desire to share the truth about losing his unborn son died on his tongue. Cassie was excited about seeing the townhouse and he didn't want to bring her down.

Besides, it suddenly hit him that he was more like her ex-husband than he wanted to admit.

Not because he hadn't wanted his son, because he had. Desperately.

But he hadn't wanted Victoria.

And in the midst of his anguish after her death he'd been unable to deny a small measure of relief to know that he wouldn't have to spend the rest of his life with her.

A fact that made him a terrible person. Not much better than Evan.

Certainly not good enough for Cassie.

* * *

Cassie felt better once she'd told Ryan the truth. And he'd been nothing but supportive.

She sensed that there were things he wanted to talk about, too, and feared he'd go into detail again about what her options were as far as having a child of her own. For some reason, she couldn't help thinking that he'd been trying to convince himself that there were other opportunities to have a child. Maybe because deep down he knew how much he wanted to have children of his own.

Maybe it was for the best that there wasn't enough time for further discussion. "I'm sorry, Ryan, but can we head over to the townhouse now? I'd like to be there a few minutes early."

"Of course," he agreed. "Buckle up."

She pulled her hair back into a ponytail and then latched her seat belt. She pulled out her phone so she could give him directions.

"Take Main Street and then turn left on Lilac Road," she said.

"Lots of kids playing around here," he commented.

She nodded, loving the fact that this area seemed ideal for raising a family. "Turn left on Lavender, and the townhouse should be right there on the corner."

"I think I see the For Sale sign," he said as they approached.

"No, that's Rosewood," she said, glancing down at the paperwork she held in her hand. "Lavender is the next block."

He nodded and continued, although she found herself thinking that the moderate-sized Cape Cod with the For Sale sign in the front yard looked inviting, too.

Way beyond her price range, though.

"There it is," she said, craning her neck to see better. "They're side-by-side townhouses. And I love how close it is to the park."

"I see it," he said, pulling over to the curb.

"It only has two bedrooms," she said, feeling self-conscious about her choice. "But that's all Emma and I really need."

"It looks great," he said as he shut off the engine.

Cassie slid out of the passenger seat, thrilled to see the townhouse up close. Granted, it was small, but she refused to let that fact get her down. Besides, the price was already a stretch since she'd have to take out a loan against her retirement plan to afford her rent and the down payment.

"The roof looks to be in good shape," Ryan said, gesturing with his hand. "And the outside appears to be low maintenance."

"So far, so good," she agreed, glad he was there to give her some pointers. "I wonder who lives next door?"

"That's a good question, since you'll be sharing the building and the yard," he said. "Maybe the Realtor knows?"

"I wish she'd get here," Cassie muttered. "I'm dying to see the inside."

"That's probably her now."

Cassie shielded her eyes against the glare of the summer sun to check out the car that had turned onto the street. Sure enough, the driver was a woman who looked like the photograph of Andrea Langley she'd seen on the website. "I'm glad she came early, too."

Andrea parked the car in front of the townhouse and slid out from the driver's seat. Cassie met her halfway.

"Thanks for coming on short notice," she said, holding out her hand to Andrea.

"My pleasure," Andrea said with a broad smile. She glanced over at Ryan. "Nice to see you, too, Dr. Murphy."

Cassie's eyebrows lifted in surprise. "I didn't realize you knew each other."

"I've listed my house with Andrea," Ryan said.

Really? Why on earth hadn't he mentioned that fact? But this wasn't the time or the place to ask. Especially as Andrea began talking about the property.

"The inside needs a little work," Andrea warned, as she unlocked the front door, "but a little paint and new carpeting will make it look as good as new."

Cassie's excitement faded to despair when she saw what Andrea meant. The walls must have been white once, but now had an icky brown tinge to them. The interior reeked of stale cigarette smoke, which made her gag. Maybe paint and pulling the old carpeting out might help, but what if that didn't work? She felt certain an entire can of air freshener wouldn't make a dent in the stench.

"It's worse than it looks on the website," Cassie said, breathing through her nose as she turned to Andrea. "I'm not sure if I'll have enough money to fix it up."

Andrea's smile slipped as she nodded. "I understand, but you could try a low offer, see if the sellers would be willing to move on the price."

"Maybe," Cassie agreed, glancing around the living room and kitchen area. Andrea threw open a few windows while she walked down the hall to the two bedrooms, which were small but serviceable.

"There's a half basement, too, where the washer and

dryer are located," Andrea pointed out cheerfully, obviously trying to salvage her potential sale. "And the appliances are included."

"That helps," Cassie acknowledged, trying to battle a wave of depression. She couldn't imagine bringing Emma into this place as it was now.

"The foundation looks sound," Ryan pointed out, as they walked around the basement. "The basics are all here, so Andrea is right, it's just a matter of adding paint and carpeting."

"Absolutely," Andrea agreed, as they trooped back up to the main level. "What do you think, Cassie?"

Honestly, she wasn't sure what to think. Disappointment stabbed deep but she did her best to try and be optimistic. "It has potential, but the price would have to be at least twelve grand lower to make up for what I'd have to put into this to make it livable."

Andrea winced and then shrugged. "Well, it can't hurt to try," she said. "Maybe they'll counter and we can meet in the middle."

"I'm not sure I can afford much more," Cassie said frankly. "I have maybe a few thousand in wiggle room, but that's about all. If they'll accept a lower offer, then I can pay for the upgrades and the rent for the duration of my lease."

Andrea nodded, although her expression reflected her discouragement. "All right, I'll put the offer together before you have to go to work."

Cassie looked around the interior again, noting that the open windows didn't help the smell. Andrea was right, the place had potential, but the thought of doing all the work to make it worthwhile was a bit daunting.

"Do you know anything about the Cape Cod for sale

on Rosewood?" Ryan asked. "That one has definite curb appeal."

Cassie glanced at him, wondering at his sudden decision to list his house. "Why are you interested in moving?"

He shrugged. "The place I have now is too big for me and isn't really to my taste."

She was surprised to hear that, mostly because the timing seemed off. After all, his wife had been dead for three years. Why the sudden desire to move now, after all this time?

Had investigating Trey's overdose caused his old feelings for his wife to resurface? Maybe, but he'd also said that her death had been his fault.

And she realized that even though they'd bonded over Emma and had made love, there was a chance that Ryan still wasn't ready for a more permanent type of relationship.

As kind and supportive as he'd been when she'd told him about her inability to have children, he hadn't mentioned that he didn't care.

In fact, he might secretly be disappointed in her inability to carry a child, but hadn't said anything out of kindness. Maybe, in his mind, she wasn't the right woman for him.

And she realized that it was entirely possible that she cared about him far more than he cared for her.

CHAPTER THIRTEEN

RYAN FELT TERRIBLE that Cassie's excitement over her townhouse had been crushed by the work that was needed inside. The place did have potential, but it would take a lot of elbow grease and money to make it a home.

And for some reason he couldn't get the Cape Cod house out of his mind.

But there was plenty of time to worry about that later. Right now he was more concerned about Cassie. As he drove her back to her apartment, her despair was evident on her face. "I can help you with the townhouse," he offered.

"Thanks, but first we have to find out if the sellers will drop the price," she said with a sad smile.

"Things will work out," he said encouragingly. Trying to keep his distance from her wasn't working too well. "You'll see."

"I hope so," she said wistfully, as she pushed open the passenger door. "Thanks again, Ryan."

Knowing she had to work, he forced himself to let her go. "Take care, Cassie."

He watched her walk toward her car, wishing he could make her feel better. But then his phone rang and he jumped on it, recognizing Detective Trammel's number. "This is Ryan Murphy."

"Dr. Murphy, I have good news. We've linked Oliver Stevenson to several other prescription drugs that have been filled here in Wisconsin. We're in the process of working with the Feds to bring him in."

"Really?" He tried to comprehend what Trammel was saying. "You think that he'll pay for his crimes?"

"I do. We found another strip-mall office of his and sent in an undercover cop with cash. The cop came out with a prescription for a month's supply of oxycodone. Unfortunately, the doc himself wasn't there, but it's just a matter of time. We're in the process of solidifying our case against him."

Relief was overwhelming. "Thank you for telling me," Ryan managed. "I'm glad he'll finally be brought to justice."

"Me, too," Trammel echoed. "And I'm sorry I didn't take your concerns more seriously back when your wife died."

That much was true, and he didn't want to think about how many deaths had occurred in the past three years as a result. But at least they could stop this guy moving forward. "It's okay, just make sure you get him into custody and soon."

"We will. Take care, Dr. Murphy."

Trammel disconnected from the call, leaving Ryan staring at his phone, still reeling from shock. It was over. So why didn't he feel better? Wasn't this the justice he'd sought?

Of course it was.

Yet he knew that arresting Oliver Stevenson wouldn't bring his son back.

And the guilt that had plagued him over the past three years hadn't lessened much at all.

He scrubbed his hands over his face. Maybe the first step was to confide in Cassie. She was working, but he wasn't. Maybe he could meet her for dinner? Or wait to talk to her at the end of her shift?

Either way, the need to talk to Cassie couldn't be denied. Maybe she could give him the absolution he couldn't seem to give himself.

Cassie swiped in at work and immediately crossed over to Emma's warmer. Her mouth dropped open in surprise when she discovered Emma had been taken off the ventilator a few hours prior to the start of her shift. Even the feeding tube was gone.

"Oh, sweetpea, you look wonderful," she whispered. The baby appeared to be asleep, with only a reddened area on her cheek from where the feeding tube had been held in place remaining as a sign of what she'd been through.

Tears pricked her eyes at how wonderful Emma looked not being connected to a ventilator.

"Hey, are you ready for our bedside shift report?" Diane asked, crossing over to Emma's warmer.

"Absolutely," Cassie agreed. "Although I can already see how much progress little Emma has made."

"Yes, although we're still keeping a close eye on her for signs of apnea. And she'll need to be fed soon, so let's finish up. Are you taking care of Daniel, too?" When Cassie nodded, Diane smiled. "Great, then this won't take too long."

Cassie concentrated on listening to the detailed information Diane gave her, even though it wasn't easy.

It was shocking to realize how much she wanted to call Ryan to share the good news about Emma.

Daniel was also doing much better and she finished her assessment just as he began to wake up. His parents were coming in to feed him, but he was cranky with having to wait, so she picked him up and walked around the nursery, trying to soothe him.

When his parents arrived, his mother rushed over. "Oh, thank you for waiting, although I feel terrible that we didn't get here sooner."

She smiled as she handed Daniel over to his mother. "It's been less than ten minutes, so don't worry, he's fine."

Cassie made sure that Daniel's parents were settled in to feed him before heading over to Emma's warmer. The baby still looked peaceful, but she was starting to squirm around a bit, indicating that she might wake up soon.

And no doubt would be as hungry as Daniel had been.

Diane had mentioned that Emma had taken her first bottle feeding just two hours ago, but it wasn't uncommon for babies to eat more frequently after being under stress. Plus, the little girl had only taken two ounces, so it wasn't surprising she needed more in her tummy.

Cassie quickly put a bottle together for Emma, sensing she was on borrowed time. When Emma let out a plaintive wail, Cassie smiled, thinking that even Emma's cry sounded good after days of silence while she'd been supported on the ventilator.

"There, now, I'm here, sweetpea," she murmured as she began changing Emma's diaper. When that task was finished she quickly washed her hands and then picked the baby up, nestling the little girl against her shoulder. Emma's crying grew louder and more insistent so Cassie turned the baby so that Emma was propped in the crook of her arm and sat down in the rocking chair to feed her.

At that exact moment she looked up to find Ryan standing there, wearing casual nonwork clothes and staring at her, his deeply intent gaze making her shiver with awareness.

And just that quickly the memories of their lovemaking came rushing back, at the worst possible moment. She'd never experienced anything like making love with Ryan, and Cassie knew she needed to look away before everyone noticed the emotion shimmering in her eyes. But it wasn't easy. Only when Emma reached up to put her tiny hand on top of Cassie's hand holding the bottle did she find the strength to break the connection.

She tried to get her bearings, as Ryan came even closer. Telling herself to ignore him was impossible, but she did her best, gazing down at Emma, who sucked at the bottle like a pro.

"Isn't she beautiful?" she whispered, finding the nerve to glance up at him.

"Yes. And so are you," Ryan said in a low husky tone. Thankfully no one was standing right next to them.

Still, she felt her cheeks grow warm, knowing the other staff members were likely glancing at them curiously. "What are you doing here?" she asked in a whisper. "Did you come to see Emma?"

He slowly shook his head. "No, but I'm thrilled to see she's off the vent. I came to see you. I realize you're working but will you have dinner with me when you have time for a break?"

She wanted to refuse outright, but her tongue didn't seem to be working properly. "We have a woman who's in preterm labor," she finally managed. "I'm not sure I'll get a dinner break during my shift."

"I'll wait," he said, obviously unwilling to accept any excuse. "And if you don't have time, then I'll wait until after your shift is over."

She stared at him helplessly. "Why?"

"Because I need to talk to you. Please? It's important."

The earnest expression in his eyes made it impossible for Cassie to refuse his request. "All right, but keep in mind that dinner isn't likely."

"That's okay. I'll swing by and if you're too busy I'll come back later." He stroked a hand over Emma's downy hair before turning to leave.

She watched him go, the urge to call him back nearly overwhelming. She focused her gaze on Emma instead. She knew that Ryan wanted to explain why he'd claimed that his wife's death had been his fault, and he deserved to be heard.

And with the way her pulse rate had tripled on seeing him again, she suspected that nothing he could say would change her feelings about him.

She cared about Ryan, more than she could ever articulate.

Was it possible he felt the same way? Or had their amazing night of passion been one-sided? Did he wish for someone different? Someone who could bear him the children he deserved?

Or was fostering children enough?

She gave herself a mental shake, knowing that she'd have her answers soon enough. Right now, Emma needed her attention.

After the baby finished one ounce, Cassie gently took the bottle away and held Emma against her shoulder, rubbing the baby's back to encourage a burp. The sound was little more than a hiccup, but did the trick.

It was so amazing to watch Emma drink from a bottle, without having any tubes. The baby didn't even have the IV anymore, although the tiny bruises where the needles had been still lingered. No doubt Emma would soon be moved to the level-two nursery, which was one step closer to being discharged.

For a moment her heart squeezed in her breast. She was thrilled the baby was making progress, but at the same time, Emma's well-being was more proof that she might not be able to become a foster parent in time.

Fate might have other plans for Emma.

Plans that didn't include *her*.

For all she knew, there was a couple out there who would take Emma in and provide the baby with both a mother and a father. After all, Emma's medical needs were probably not nearly as bad as they'd initially feared.

A two-parent household would always take precedence over a single parent, like herself, even if she was given an exception for her one-bedroom apartment.

But she refused to let that selfish thought ruin her day. If Emma wasn't meant for her, then so be it. Having Emma move up to the level-two nursery was a huge accomplishment.

Normally Cassie cared for the sicker babies, but maybe her boss would make an exception. If not, she'd still rejoice in the news that Emma was getting better. Because Emma's health was all that mattered.

The baby's heath and finding a loving family to take care of her.

Ryan was disappointed when he learned that the neonatal unit was short-staffed over the dinner hour, thanks to a preemie delivery, so Cassie wasn't free to meet him.

He returned toward the end of her shift and she looked surprised to see him waiting there. She smiled and crossed over. "You must be bored out of your mind with nothing to do during my entire shift."

"Not at all," he said, although the waiting had been pure torture. "Are you hungry? Did you get a chance to eat anything?"

"Yes, I'm hungry and, no, I didn't get a chance to eat dinner. It's been crazy. We had two preemies deliver right after each other."

He thought for a minute. "We can either eat in the cafeteria or at San Flippo's Pizzeria right across the street."

"Pizza sounds wonderful."

As they walked toward the elevator, he rested his hand in the small of her back, needing the brief physical connection. Watching her feed Emma had made him realize how much he cared about Cassie.

And emphasized just how important this conversation would be.

"Any news on the townhouse?" he asked, as they rode the elevator down to the lobby level.

She grimaced and shrugged. "They countered but only dropped the price three grand, so it's not looking good."

Once again, he thought about the Cape Cod located near the park. But he was getting way ahead of himself. First they needed to talk. A heavy conversation that might be better with food in their stomachs.

"I'm sorry, Cassie," he murmured.

"It's all right. Emma's doing so much better, anyway, that I'm sure other foster parents will step forward to claim her."

He wanted to reassure her, but unfortunately she was right. Emma's medical needs might not be a barrier after all.

But deep down he knew that Emma and Cassie belonged together.

The walk across the street to San Flippo's didn't take long, and he had to smile when Cassie ordered a pizza with the works, just the way he liked it.

"Let's sit in the back," he said, choosing an isolated area of the eating space on purpose.

They took a seat as the server came over with their soft drinks. "The pizza will be ready soon."

"I hope so, because I'm starving," she muttered, half under her breath.

He couldn't help but grin. "Should I get an order of breadsticks to tide you over?"

She wrinkled her nose at him. "No, thanks. I'd rather eat the real deal."

He nodded. "Okay, we'll wait."

She played with her straw wrapper. "Ryan, why did you want to talk to me so badly that you couldn't wait until tomorrow?"

He cleared his throat, wondering where to start. "I heard from Detective Trammel after I dropped you off at your apartment. They've arrested Dr. Oliver Stevenson for running illegal drug clinics."

Cassie's eyes widened in shock. "Really? Trey got his prescription filled there?"

He nodded. "Yeah, and apparently this doc moved around a lot, slapping up clinics in strip malls and other cheap business rental places and then tearing them down to move again. But he won't hurt anyone else. He's done."

"Oh, Ryan, I'm so happy for you." Cassie reached over to cover his hand in hers. "I'm sure this must be a huge relief."

"Thanks." He knew he had to tell her the rest, but at that moment their server showed up with their pizza.

"Yum, that looks delicious." Cassie helped herself to a generous slice, so he did the same.

They ate in silence for several minutes as he tried to figure out how to confess the rest of the story to Cassie.

As it turned out, she brought it up first.

"Ryan, if the police arrested the doctor who supplied your wife's pills, why do you feel responsible for her death?"

The pizza he'd eaten sat like a lump of dough in his gut. He gulped down some water before lifting his gaze to meet hers.

"I didn't love Victoria the way I should have," he finally said. "We were young, too young to realize what we were getting into. Victoria liked being a doctor's wife and was obsessed with her looks, to the point of weighing herself every single morning and freaking out if she gained a half a pound."

Cassie pushed her empty plate away, her gaze never wavering from his. "Go on," she encouraged.

He licked suddenly dry lips. "I was thinking about filing for divorce—in fact, I'd already met with a lawyer to begin the process. But that evening, when I came home, Victoria told me she was pregnant."

She gasped, so loudly that he was surprised the few patrons of the restaurant didn't turn around to see what was going on. "She was pregnant?" she whispered.

The pizza congealed in his gut. "Yeah. I was thrilled about the baby and decided to forget about the divorce. My parents divorced when I was young and I was shuffled between them for most of my early life. I didn't want that for my son." He let out a heavy sigh. "But I didn't know Victoria was still taking prescription painkillers. She'd had surgery a year earlier, and it never occurred to me that she'd become addicted to them."

Cassie didn't say a word, her eyes wide with horror. He forced himself to finish it.

"Don't you see? I was clueless. I didn't know she was taking pills. And I can't help thinking that she used them as a crutch because I didn't love her enough."

He tossed his napkin over his plate with a wave of self-disgust. "When Victoria died of an accidental drug overdose, she took my son along with her. And as much as I missed him, there was a tiny part of me that was relieved she was gone."

Cassie stared at him for a long moment before she tore her gaze away. "I don't know what to say," she whispered. "I had no idea…"

Her voice trailed off and the way she wouldn't look at him only cemented the truth.

She was appalled by his actions. And obviously didn't want anything to do with him now that she knew.

And, worst of all, he couldn't blame her.

CHAPTER FOURTEEN

CASSIE PRESSED HER shaking hands together as she rose to her feet. "Excuse me," she said in a strangled tone before making her way to the woman's restroom. For long moments she stood, her hands braced on the countertop, trying to get a grip on her emotions.

Ryan had lost his son. A son he'd wanted desperately enough to try to make his loveless marriage work.

He'd lost his son!

Cassie took several deep breaths, trying to calm herself. After she'd told him about her two miscarriages and the need to have surgery, Ryan hadn't mentioned anything about losing his son.

To be fair, she hadn't given him a chance, since she'd been anxious to see the townhouse.

Still, it was clear that she might never be able to give Ryan the son he wanted. Sure, he'd been supportive of her quest to become a foster mother for Emma, and had claimed that there were many other options available to have children. But he'd want a son of his own.

She loved him. She loved him and he clearly deserved the chance to have his own child. No matter what he might say to the contrary.

Her instincts weren't reliable when it came to men.

"Cassandra? Are you all right?"

Hearing Ryan's voice on the other side of the door made tears spring to her eyes. She quickly splashed cold water on her face to hide the evidence and to bring some color back into her pale face.

She walked out of the restroom, surprised he'd come to see if she was all right. "I'm fine and I shouldn't have left you like that. I'm sorry, Ryan. So sorry for everything you've been through."

He stared at her, his gaze impassive. She couldn't figure out what he was thinking. "I've already paid the bill, so I'll drive you home."

She was surprised he wanted the evening to end so soon, especially after he'd waited her entire shift to talk to her. But then again, she'd left to pull herself together. "I'm sorry," she said again. "And my car is at the hospital."

"Then I'll take you to your car."

She followed him outside, still shaken by the news that he'd lost his son but feeling terrible that she'd reacted so badly. Why had she made it about her own loss, instead of supporting Ryan?

"Her death wasn't your fault," she murmured, as he drove back across the street to the hospital parking lot.

"Yeah, right." His sarcastic tone bit deep.

"Listen, Ryan, I'm not an expert, but I'm sure your wife tried to keep her addiction a secret."

"That isn't the point."

She wasn't sure what the point was, but he didn't say anything more as he pulled up alongside her car. She sat for a moment, trying to think of some way to ease his guilt.

"Goodnight, Cassie."

The finality of his tone couldn't be ignored. "Goodnight, Ryan," she murmured, her heart aching for him as she slid out of his car to climb into hers.

Ryan drove away without so much as a backward glance.

And she knew, with sick certainty, that he'd never love her the way she loved him. How could he? He wouldn't be able to love anyone until he learned to forgive himself.

Ryan kept seeing the horrified expression in Cassie's eyes over and over again. She'd tried to tell him that Victoria's death hadn't been his fault, but she hadn't mentioned anything about the way he'd been secretly relieved that he hadn't been stuck with Victoria for the rest of his life.

A statement that had sent her running to the bathroom so she could pull herself together in private.

He couldn't sleep and was glad to know that he wasn't scheduled to work the next day. Not that he'd mind keeping busy, but he wouldn't do his tiny patients any good coming in to work sleep deprived.

The thought of his infant patients reminded him of Emma. Beautiful Emma, who'd looked adorable in Cassie's arms.

He tried to slam the door on those images but they kept rolling through his mind like a movie that wouldn't end.

His heart squeezed painfully in his chest as he realized how much he loved Cassie.

He loved her.

But she would never return his feelings.

Somehow he must have dozed a bit because suddenly

the early morning sunshine woke him up. He blinked and rolled out of bed with a low groan.

Maybe he should offer to work today. There were three neonatal intensivists and between them they covered the unit 24/7. Erica Ryerson was on today, and since she'd asked off for the past weekend he knew she'd insist on staying.

Which meant he had a long, endless day stretching ahead of him.

Ryan's phone rang and his pulse leaped as he grabbed his phone, but of course the caller wasn't Cassie. He answered it halfheartedly. "Hello?"

"Dr. Murphy? Andrea Langley here. First of all, I have a couple interested in looking at your house this afternoon. Isn't that fantastic?"

He rubbed the back of his neck, trying to garner some enthusiasm. "Yeah, that's great. What time?"

"Two o'clock. But I was also wondering if there were any properties you were interested in seeing? You might want to pick something out in case we get lucky and someone puts in an offer on your place."

The Cape Cod located next to the park flashed into his mind, although his previous excitement about the place had waned considerably.

"Sure, why not?" He mentioned the house he had in mind. At least seeing it would give him something to do. "I can meet you there in an hour or so, if that works?"

"Perfect. See you then."

He disconnected from the call, forcing himself to take a shower, change and grab something to eat before heading over to the house he'd glimpsed yesterday when he'd driven Cassie to the townhouse.

Seeing the Cape Cod up close only reinforced his

belief that the place would be perfect for Cassie. For Cassie and Emma, or any other baby she decided to foster.

The thawed spot in his heart ached to the point he pressed his hand to the center of his chest in a vain effort to ease the pain. This was why he'd held himself closed off from everyone since Victoria's death.

Because love hurt too damn much.

He hadn't loved Victoria enough, but he'd loved his son. And losing his baby boy had gutted him.

Now he felt the same way over losing Cassie.

Andrea babbled on and on about the house, but all he could see was Cassie everywhere he looked. Cassie in the kitchen, the bedroom. Holding Emma. Holding their child.

"Well? What do you think?" Andrea asked.

He nodded, wondering if he'd see Cassie in every house he viewed. "It's nice."

"Are you interested in putting in an offer?" she asked, not seeming to notice his lackluster attitude.

"Let me think about it a bit more," he hedged. "After all, this is the first house I've looked at."

Andrea looked disappointed, but she nodded. "Okay, do you have other places in mind?"

He didn't have a clue. And it was difficult to drum up the energy to care. "I'll make a list and get back to you," he promised.

Andrea wasn't thrilled, but he didn't care. He walked back out to his car, tempted to take a long drive along the coast of Lake Michigan.

But doing that only reminded him again of Cassie. The way she enjoyed riding in his convertible. The way she'd tipped her face up to the sun. The way she laughed.

As he drove home, he realized that he'd never be able to forget all the memories he'd shared with Cassie.

When he pulled into his driveway, there was a car parked in front of his house. It took him a minute to realize the sedan belonged to Cassie.

A mixture of dread and pleasure filled his chest. He must be a glutton for punishment, because even knowing that all she wanted to do was to rehash everything from last night, he was still happy to see her.

"Hi," she greeted him awkwardly.

He tried, and failed, to summon a smile. "Cassie. What brings you here?"

"I didn't sleep very well last night," she said.

"Me, either," he admitted. "And don't worry, I understand."

Her brow knitted in confusion. "Understand what?"

"Why you ran off to the bathroom like that." He glanced around, thinking that standing in his driveway probably wasn't the best place to have this conversation. "Do you want to go inside?"

She hesitated. "Could we take a walk instead?"

"Sure." The fact that she didn't want to be inside Victoria's house wasn't too surprising. He fell into step beside her as they made their way down to the road.

"I shouldn't have run to the bathroom last night," she said. "I'm sorry. Hearing about how you lost a son similar to the way I lost two babies hit me harder than I expected."

He was surprised to hear that. "I figured you were upset about the fact that I was secretly glad to be free of Victoria." There, he'd said it again, in case she hadn't heard him the first time.

"Oh, Ryan, I know just how that feels. As much as I mourned the loss of my baby, I was also secretly glad to know that I found out about Evan, too. I wanted my child more than anything, but sharing that child with someone like him…" She shrugged. "It took me a long time to realize that maybe losing my baby was a mixed blessing."

He was flabbergasted by her admission. "You don't think I'm a terrible person?" he asked.

She frowned. "Of course not."

The relief that hit him was overwhelming. "You don't know how much hearing that means to me." He captured her hand in his and stopped so he could face her. "I'm glad you don't hate me."

Her eyes filled with compassion. "I don't hate you, Ryan. I can't hate you when I've fallen in love with you."

His mouth dropped open in surprise and the stabbing pain in his heart eased. "Cassandra, I love you, too."

He would have kissed her but she threw up her hand, planting it in the center of his chest. "I'm sorry, but I find that hard to believe," she said huskily. "How can you love me when you haven't forgiven yourself?"

He covered her hand on his chest with his. "Cassie, you have to understand that I've been trying to forgive myself since the day Victoria died."

Her smile was sad. "I know, and I suspect that finding that Dr. Stevenson, who'd supplied her pain meds, helped a bit."

"Yes, but that wasn't the biggest change that helped me," he said, gazing down into her wide brown eyes.

He needed her to believe him. "It was you, Cassandra. All you. Your warmth, your laughter, your smile. After I lost my son, I refused to care that much about anyone. You healed the piece of my heart that I thought was lost forever."

"Oh, Ryan," she whispered. "I want so badly to believe you."

He understood that trust must be difficult, considering the way her ex had betrayed her. "What can I say to make you believe me? I love you so much. I love you and I want to be with you, forever."

Amazing how saying the words became easier and easier when they were right.

"You realize I probably can't give you children," she said, dropping her gaze. "I'll have the surgery, but there are no guarantees. And even though I probably won't get to foster Emma, I'd still like to complete the classes, just in case another baby comes along that needs a home."

"Of course you'll complete the classes," Ryan said. He gently tipped her chin up so that he could look into her eyes. "I love you, Cassandra. Babies, either foster-care babies or our own, will just be an added bonus. Don't you see? You're the most important person to me."

"How can you be so sure?" she asked.

He cupped her face in his hands. "Because you hold the tiny piece of my heart that I thought was frozen forever. Without you, I'm nothing but a shell of a man going through the motions of life. Emma may have brought us together initially, but you're the one who healed my heart. You healed my soul. I will always love you, so if you need time, I'll wait for as long as it takes. And I'll never hurt you. Because anything that upsets you hurts me worse."

Tears filled her eyes and he couldn't help himself.

He kissed her, trying to reinforce without words just how much she meant to him.

Cassie wrapped her arms around Ryan's neck, drowning in the sweetness of his kiss.

Was it possible that he really had forgiven himself? And if so, could she trust in his feelings for her? Trust him when he claimed that her ability to give him a child didn't matter?

A car horn honked, breaking them apart from their heated kiss.

"How about I drive us back to your place?" Ryan asked in a husky voice. "I need to be with you. Even if all we do is talk some more."

"I'd like that," she murmured. He'd promised to give her time, but right now she couldn't bear to be separated from him, either.

The expression of love in his eyes couldn't be faked. And if he loved her, then he surely accepted her the way she was, right? Faults and all.

The same way she loved him.

They walked back to his place and he insisted on leaving her car there so they could take the convertible. "We'll come back to get it later."

She nodded, thinking that right now she was feeling too emotional to drive anyway. Thankfully she still had the hair tie so she could pull her hair back in a ponytail.

"Um, Ryan? This isn't the way to my apartment," she said when he turned left instead of right.

"I know, but I have something I'd like to show you."

The smile on his face dazzled her. He looked so different from the aloof physician she'd first met when she'd moved here six months ago.

When he turned on Rosewood, she recognized the Cape Cod. "It's adorable," she said. "Are you thinking of buying it?"

He shrugged and glanced at her. "That depends on you."

"Me?" Her heart leaped into her throat.

"Yes, you. I'll give you all the time you need to believe how much I love you, but I refuse to buy a house you don't like. So whether or not I buy this house depends on you."

Cassie unbuckled her seat belt and threw herself into his arms. "Yes," she whispered. "Yes, I like this house. But I love you more."

This time their sizzling kiss wasn't easy to break off. "We need to get to your place," he muttered. "As soon as possible."

She couldn't help giggling as she buckled herself back in. Thankfully Cedar Bluff wasn't too big a town and they reached her apartment building in a few minutes.

And when Ryan tugged her toward the bedroom, she gladly followed him.

Cassie wanted nothing more than to spend the day in bed with Ryan, but when her phone rang for the third time, she decided she'd better answer it.

"Where are you going?" Ryan asked in a husky, sated tone, capturing her hand in his.

She smiled at him, still amazed at the fact that he loved her. And had gone to great lengths to prove it over the past two hours. "I need to get the phone, that's the third time it's gone off."

"I didn't hear it," he admitted, with a sexy smile. "I was too busy kissing every inch of your delectable body."

The urge to forget the stupid phone to crawl back next to him was strong, but she couldn't quite ignore the niggling worry. She dropped a quick kiss on his mouth. "I'll be right back," she promised.

"All right."

She felt self-conscious parading around naked, so she grabbed his T-shirt off the floor and pulled it over her head, grateful it was long enough to cover her bare bottom. She remembered leaving her phone on the kitchen counter and when she picked it up her heart leapt into her throat when she saw five missed calls from Lydia.

Five? She'd only heard it ring three times!

She quickly pushed the button to return the call, practically holding her breath. The older woman picked up on the second ring. "Hello?"

"Lydia, it's me, Cassie. I'm sorry I missed your calls. What's wrong? Are you okay? Did something happen to Emma?"

"Oh, Cassie, I'm so glad you returned my call. I wanted to tell you the news myself."

She frowned, trying to clear her sex-fogged mind. "What news?" Ryan appeared at her side wearing nothing but his boxers, looking so sexy, she momentarily forgot who she was talking to. Oh, yes, Lydia. She forced herself to peel her gaze away from Ryan and to focus on the call.

"I've talked to Avery and both she and her boyfriend are going to sign off on their parental rights to Emma."

Cassie knew that signing away parental rights meant that the adoption process would go faster, but obviously Lydia didn't know that she wasn't going to be able to foster Emma after all.

"That's great news, Lydia," she said, trying to inject enthusiasm in her tone. "I'm sure Emma's foster parents will be thrilled."

"What do you mean?" Lydia asked. "I thought you were fostering Emma?"

"I was, but—" She stopped, looking up at Ryan, who'd joined her. "I might not be able to get everything finished in time."

"Are you sure?" The disappointed note in Lydia's voice stabbed deep. "I was feeling so much better knowing that Emma was going to be living with you."

"And I want Emma, too. All I can promise is to do my best. But are you sure Avery and her boyfriend are really okay with this? After all, everyone deserves a second chance."

"Absolutely sure," Lydia assured her. "Avery knows that she has a long road ahead of her and is willing to go into rehab. Her boyfriend has agreed to go, too. And, honestly, she just wants the baby to go to a good home. And we'd like that to be with you."

"I'll try," Cassie said with a misty smile. "Goodbye, Lydia."

"We'll do more than try," Ryan said firmly, when she set her phone aside. "We'll do everything possible to get custody of Emma."

"Really?" Cassie's gaze was full of hope.

"Yes, really." Ryan's grin lit up his entire face and he picked her up so that her feet weren't even on the floor, twirling around until they were both dizzy, whispering into her ear how much he loved her.

"I love you, too," she managed.

"God, Cassie, just thinking of the possibility of adopting Emma is like a miracle," he said in awe. "Maybe together we can make this work."

"I know." She gazed up at Ryan, her heart melting at the moisture in the corners of his eyes. "Your love is my miracle, too, Ryan. I don't need extra time. I know how much I love you."

"And I love you, Cassandra." He cupped her face in his hands and gently kissed her. "Will you please marry me?"

"Yes, I'd love to marry you," she managed, before he kissed her again.

They ended up back in her bedroom, giggling and laughing as they made love. When they'd finished, she gathered the last remnants of energy to prop herself on her elbow, so she could gaze down at Ryan. "So, how about you take me over to see the inside of that house you picked out for us?"

A shadow crossed his features. "If you don't like it, we can choose something else."

"Don't be silly," she admonished him. "I already love the neighborhood, remember? And I really love the fact that it's located so close to the park. Besides, if you like the place, I'm sure I will, too. The house is just a structure, but it's the people inside that make it a home."

"I'm the luckiest man in the world. You've filled the void in my life, Cassie," he said huskily. "With love and with laughter."

"Always," she promised, knowing that he'd returned

the favor tenfold. With Ryan and whatever children they were fortunate enough to have, she was thrilled to have the love of a good man and the family she'd always wanted.

EPILOGUE

Ten months later...

CASSIE WATCHED RYAN pushing Emma in the baby swing at the park, basking in the sound of the little girl's giggles. After Emma's initial struggles she had grown by leaps and bounds beneath their loving care. Emma was a little delayed at first, but she was coming along every day. And they were both happy that Aunt Lydia remained a part of the baby's life.

Emma was already calling Lydia "Nanna." And if all went well, their adoption of the little girl would be complete by the end of the month.

Cassie put a protective hand over her swollen belly, loving the feel of the baby moving around inside her. She and Ryan had been doubly blessed, first, having been able to adopt Emma and, second, when she'd successfully gone through the recommended surgery and had become pregnant.

"Are you all right?" Ryan asked in concern. He took Emma out of her swing and crossed over to her.

"I'm fine. Our baby is just a bit active today," she assured him, taking Emma into her arms. "Did you have fun with Daddy?" she asked.

"Dada," Emma agreed. The she nestled against Cassie. "Mama."

Hearing Emma speak was a huge blessing and she couldn't help tears gathering in her eyes. Then again, it could be the fact that her hormones were a bit out of control.

"I love you, too, sweetpea," she said, pressing a kiss to Emma's plump cheek.

"Maybe you should go home to rest," Ryan said, worry creasing his brow. Ever since she'd told him she was expecting, he'd become more protective than a papa bear.

Not that she blamed him. At first they'd both feared another miscarriage, but now that she was just past twenty weeks she was breathing easier. And she reveled in Ryan's love and attention.

Ryan held her close every single night that he wasn't working, reassuring her that, no matter what happened, he still loved her. And he often talked to her belly, telling the baby how much they loved him or her ,and how much they wanted him or her to grow healthy and strong.

"Are you sure you don't regret jumping into marriage and babies so fast?" Ryan asked, as he gently took Emma back into his arms so Cassie wouldn't have to carry the added weight as they turned toward home. She'd fallen in love with the Cape Cod and together they'd made it a home. "I feel like I rushed you into all this."

She leaned against him, reveling in his strength. "I don't regret one minute," she said with a contented sigh. Everyone in Cedar Bluff had thought they were crazy to get married so quickly but, oddly enough, they'd wanted to be married before welcoming Emma into their lives. "You, and Emma and this new baby are all I've ever wanted."

"Does that mean you've changed your mind about finding out the sex of the baby?" he asked with a teasing grin.

"No, I want the sex of the baby to be a surprise. For both of us."

"I'm holding out for a baby sister for Emma, a little girl who looks just like you," he said, just before he kissed her.

She kissed him back, not really caring one way or the other. A little boy like Ryan would be great, but a sister for Emma would be amazing, too. Either way, she was already blessed.

All that mattered was their love for each other.

And their new family.

* * * * *

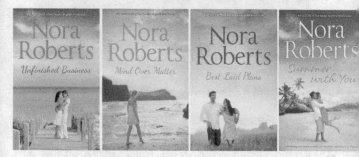

MILLS & BOON®

The Chatsfield Collection!

Style, spectacle, scandal…!

With the eight Chatsfield siblings happily married and settling down, it's time for a new generation of Chatsfields to shine, in this brand-new 8-book collection! The prospect of a merger with the Harrington family's boutique hotels will shape the future forever. But who will come out on top?

**Find out at
www.millsandboon.co.uk/TheChatsfield2**

MILLS & BOON®

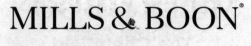

THE ULTIMATE IN ROMANTIC MEDICAL DRAMA

A sneak peek at next month's titles...

In stores from 1st May 2015:

- **Always the Midwife** – Alison Roberts *and*
  Midwife's Baby Bump – Susanne Hampton

- **A Kiss to Melt Her Heart** – Emily Forbes *and*
  Tempted by Her Italian Surgeon – Louisa George

- **Daring to Date Her Ex** – Annie Claydon
- **The One Man to Heal Her** – Meredith Webber

Available at WHSmith, Tesco, Asda, Eason, Amazon and Apple

Just can't wait?
Buy our books online a month before they hit the shops!
visit www.millsandboon.co.uk

These books are also available in eBook format!

0415/03

Join our *EXCLUSIVE* eBook club

FROM JUST £1.99 A MONTH!

Never miss a book again with our hassle-free eBook subscription.

★ Pick how many titles you want from each series with our flexible subscription

★ Your titles are delivered to your device on the first of every month

★ Zero risk, zero obligation!

There really is nothing standing in the way of you and your favourite books!

Start your eBook subscription today at www.millsandboon.co.uk/subscribe